SAWYER JACKSON
AND THE LONG LAND

BOOK ONE

BY KEVIN TUMLINSON

www.happypantsbooks.com

SAWYER JACKSON AND THE LONG LAND
BOOK ONE OF SAWYER JACKSON

Copyright © 2014 by Kevin Tumlinson

All rights reserved, published by HAPPY PANTS BOOKS
Volume 1 of Sawyer Jackson FIRST EDITION: July 2014

ISBN-10: 0692262660
ISBN-13: 978-0692262665

HAPPY PANTS BOOKS is a trademark of Kevin Tumlinson.
www.happypantsbooks.com

To Athena Cherise and Kayla Friedrich —

You two make this fun, and keep me from looking like a complete idiot. Most of the time. Everyone has their limits.

WANT TO GET ONE OF MY BEST BOOKS FOR FREE?

ONE | KNOTWORK

Gram was a sweet old lady, but God help you when she had the butcher knife in her hand.

"You're not taking him," she hissed, and she wielded the butcher knife like a sword, waving it slowly in front of her, ready to lunge any second, to stab, to slice, to kill.

But the thing in front of her, huge and black and glistening like crude oil in a humanoid form, wasn't there to be intimidated.

It was there for me.

"You're *not* taking him" she said again, louder, punctuating the air with jabs from the butcher knife.

I was eight years old, and crouched behind her. The thing in front of us kept feinting and swiping, trying to slip around Gram and get to me. It hissed and spat, its clawed hands reaching and flexing. I couldn't see its eyes. I wasn't even sure it had any. But I could feel it *looking* at me. *Glaring* at me.

Gram had the butcher knife in one hand, but in the other she had a knotwork. I'd seen her carrying these things my whole life, twisting them around her wrinkled hands, over and over. She had them woven into all of our clothes — tight little bits of stitching, hidden in a seam or a hem or under a collar. She had them woven into afghan blankets and tied into dreamcatchers and doilies, dangling from things all over the house. They'd been there my whole life.

Now, for the first time, I noticed that the thing in front of us wasn't dodging away from the butcher knife. It was cringing away from the knotwork.

"Sawyer," Gram said. "I want you to crawl away. Stay low, and stay behind me. But crawl to the shed. Get inside. Close the door and lock it, just like Gramps showed you."

"I'm scared," I said. I was still young. I didn't know what was happening, or what this thing was, or what Gram was going to do about it.

"I know, sweetie," Gram said, never taking her eyes off of the thing in front of us. "But you have to be *brave*. The shed will protect you. There's knotwork all over it. Get in there. Close the door. You'll be safe."

"But what about you?" I whined.

She laughed. "This ol' thing ain't gonna take *me* out, Sawyer. It wasn't expecting me. Thought I'd be out. Must have used a tell. I've got the tells all twisted in the knotwork. It never saw me. Now *crawl!*"

I crawled. I moved as fast as I could to the shed. There was a combination lock on it, and I turned the dial a few times. Nothing happened. "I can't remember the combination!" I cried.

"It's written on the frame, in pencil!" Gram said.

Gramps did funny things like that. What was the point of a combination lock if the combination was written right next to it? But I was glad that it was. I read it, and turned the dial, and the lock popped open. I was inside in a flash, and had the door closed and locked behind me, using a second lock on the inside. This one used a key.

I had been inside the shed hundreds of times with Gramps. It was one of my favorite places. He'd set it up like a little workshop, with a work bench that wrapped all the way around. One section of that bench was mine — he'd sectioned it out for me, and given me my own set of tools and projects to work on. There was a high, swiveling stool with a back and arms, just like his but adjusted for my height. I was proud of my workbench, babbled about it for weeks.

There were shelves reaching to the ceiling, and so many little drawers and jars and boxes filled with things I never understood. There was the usual assortment of screws and nuts and bolts and old hardware. There were plumbing fixtures and bits of pipe, reels of wire, stacks of manuals for cars and lawn equipment. And there was string and twine. Always. *Everywhere.* There must have been *miles* of it.

But most importantly, there was knotwork. Thousands of little dream catchers and braids of twine and things that defied description were tied all over the place, dangling from nails in the walls, from the rafter beams, from practically every surface. I'd seen them before, so often they were practically invisible to me. But now I noticed every one of them. With the fear running through me, and the sweat of it covering my body, my senses were up. I was hyper alert. And I saw all of the knotwork in a way I'd never seen it before. More than just twists of string and twine, I could see a sort of light coming from the knots. Like stars in a night sky — points of light dotting a black expanse. And each thread looked like golden light, too. The longer I looked, the more obvious it became. It was like looking at a network of light.

And the patterns of the knotwork — they were telling a story. I couldn't quite …

There was a thump and grunt from outside, and I snapped back to the here and now. Suddenly, my senses all on high alert, I was noticing *everything* about the shed. I hadn't realized it before, but the place had a unique smell, like a combination of engine grease and onions, and the coppery smell of old tools mingled with the rich musk of leather and the musty aroma of wooden floor planks and walls. The smell was familiar, even if I was only just noticing. It made me feel even more safe and protected here. This was a safe place.

That memory, of a workshop as a safe haven, would stick with me for the rest of my life.

From the other side of the door I could hear hissing and snarling. Occasionally I'd hear a grunt from Gram, followed by a screeching noise from the creature. Whatever that thing was, it was no match for Gram with the butcher knife. I didn't think anything could be. She was a wiz with that knife.

Knife! I thought.

I reached into the watch pocket of my jeans and pulled out the red Swiss Army knife. Gramps gave it to me for my birthday, while we were on one of our "family outings," at a fishing camp on the Brazos River. The knife was old, and the plastic handle was scratched and cracked in a couple of spots. The tools were oiled and shiny, though. The knife blade was *really* sharp — a fact I discovered while trying to whittle a perfectly good stick into a toothpick. Gramps had warned me to stop whittling toward my thumb, but I only caught on when I ended up slipping and slicing my left thumbnail off.

I screamed and cried and thrashed while Gramps held me down and Gram cleaned the wound with hydrogen peroxide before wrapping it in gauze — twisting the gauze into a small knotwork she said would "help it heal." She'd given Gramps a pretty stern lecture afterward, which he took like a man. He promised her that he'd take the knife away from me, and he did. Later, after she'd gone to bed, he came and slipped it back into my pocket, and said, "It's a shame to let a good lesson go to waste. You've learned yours, I think. And every pocket knife has to taste the blood of the one that owns it at some point. It's how they bond with you."

If that was true, I'd certainly bonded with this particular pocket knife. At the very least, I'd learned to be very careful about where that blade was facing.

Right now I held the handle in my fist, the sharp blade out and pointed at the door, ready for anything that came through there.

After a few minutes of struggle outside, I heard a noise from the door itself. There was a sort of shuffling sound, followed by a *thump*. The lock, on the inside, suddenly clicked and opened, and I felt like throwing up. As the door creaked wide, I held the knife in front of me, as ready as I could be with my heart pounding its way out of my little chest.

Gram, framed in the light of the door, frowned at me. "When did that ol' fart give you that knife back?" she said. Then sighed. "He told you about it tasting your blood, I suppose."

"Yes'm," I said.

"Well put it away, Sawyer. And when I see your Gramps I may have to let my butcher knife 'bond' with him a bit."

I cautiously folded the blade back into the handle and slid the knife back into the watch pocket of my jeans. "What … what was that thing, Gram?" I asked.

"That? Well, sweetie, that was an Ink. That's what we called them back home. But I suppose here they'd call it a 'demon' or some nonsense. Backwards place."

"An Ink? But what is it?"

"*Was*," Gram said. "It *was* an Ink, which is one of the minions of someone called Aeodymus."

She pronounced it "Ay-odd-e-muss." I wouldn't learn the spelling until later. I learned a lot of things later.

Before I could ask any more questions, Gram came into the shed, knelt in front of me, put her hands on my shoulder and checked me up and down. She frowned. "I see it," she said.

"See what?" I asked.

"The Tick." She reached out and touched the collar of my shirt. She pinched something between her nails and brought it away, holding it close to my eyes so I could see.

There, split in two by her fingernail, was a small bug. It was sort of octagonal shaped, with tiny legs that went out in all directions. It kind of reminded me of one of the little surface mount potentiometers that Gramps used in some of his electronics projects.

"That's a tick?" I asked.

"Not one from around here. It's from back home." She sighed. "We'll have to exterminate. And I'll have to weave a whole new knotwork again. Third time I've had to hide this place."

Gram was always talking like that. I never bothered asking too many questions. She would tell me things, when the time was right. She wouldn't tell me a thing, though, if she didn't want to. Pestering her would get you nowhere. She wasn't like other adults, not even Gramps. She always had something going on in her head, like she was having a conversation with someone who wasn't in the room. Every now and then she'd actually say something out loud, or laugh at some joke only she could hear.

But she wasn't crazy. I knew that for sure. She was the smartest person I'd ever known. Even smarter than Gramps, who knew *everything*.

"Come along," Gram said, standing and dusting off the front of her blouse and her jeans. She looked around and found an old rag in a small basket under the workbench. She used this to wipe down the blade of the butcher knife, and in a moment the rag was covered in an oily black goo that I hadn't seen on the blade before. But the *knife* — for a second, it didn't look like a butcher knife. Instead it looked like some kind of sword, with a longer blade and a bell-shaped guard at the hilt. I blinked and it was back to normal. Just a butcher knife. Just like the others in the kitchen. Only this one was always with Gram, tucked into the belt of her jeans as she washed dishes or shucked corn or snapped peas. I'd seen it there my whole life. It didn't strike me as unusual until now.

I'd have to ask her about it later. For now, we wandered back into the house, with a basket of laundry quickly pulled down from the line.

That night I dreamt of Inks and golden threads and tiny ticks that followed me everywhere. And within a day or so, everything about this seemed like that — just a dream I had when I was small.

That was a long time ago — almost nine years. And even though there were strange things happening here and there, nothing quite like that happened again, and eventually I more or less forgot about Inks and butcher knives that look like swords. Eventually I just stopped thinking about it, and stopped sleeping with the Swiss Army knife clenched in my fist. Eventually I settled into the business of being a kid.

For the most part, my childhood was normal. Though, looking back, I know now that it wasn't all *that* normal. I just didn't know any better.

It never really occurred to me that I wasn't doing the sorts of things other kids did. I wasn't going to a school, for starters. I knew about them, knew that kids sometimes went there, sometimes ditched and snuck down to the river instead. But that was something *other* kids did. For me, school wasn't a place you went, it was something that *happened*. I'd wake up in the mornings and while Gram fixed eggs and sausage and big bowls of fruit for breakfast, she'd drill me. Before putting even a bite of food in my mouth I had to answer math problems and recite poems and talk about historic events. I had to talk about geography, not just naming countries and capitals but describing the primary industry and local economy. I had to discuss geology and climate. I had to talk about subatomic particles and the Heisenberg Uncertainty Principle.

I met a local kid once — a neighbor. He was in the woods that stretched for miles in every direction around our house. He was out wandering, just hiking and exploring a mile or two away from his house. We talked and climbed trees together, and he was nice. But he never understood anything I was talking about. All he knew was basic arithmetic and the names of the Presidents, and not really all of those. He'd never even heard of Heisenberg.

"How come I have to learn all this stuff when they don't teach it in school?" I asked Gram one morning.

"Grammar," she said, shooting me a look.

I sighed. "Why do I have to learn things that are not taught in school?" I asked.

She smiled, and continued washing dishes. "Well, your Gramps hasn't done you any favors with his tendency for laid back speech. But I suppose it serves to keep you undercover," she said, shaking her head as she scrubbed dried egg from a plate.

"So how come?" I asked again, just to annoy her.

"Schools *should* teach these things," she said. "But they don't. There are a lot of reasons. Teachers are overworked and underpaid. Too many students per teacher. Too many requirements, decided by a school board that has no idea what 'education' really is. But mostly, I think there's an agenda to keep the population stupid."

Gram was always saying things like that.

"But you're telling me why the schools *don't* teach it," I said. "You're not answering my question. I want to know why I have to learn these things, even when other kids don't have to."

I caught the slight smile before she hid it, and I knew I had her. She and Gramps had taught me how to listen, not just hear. People say more with what they don't say, they'd told me.

"You're different than those other kids," she said. "In a way that the schools would never understand. You'd end up in trouble all the time, because you'd be bored and looking for things to do to keep yourself occupied. You'd end up causing trouble, and schools just want kids to sit and do what they're told, keep their mouths shut, and definitely *not* cause trouble."

"How would I cause trouble?" I asked.

"By being *you*, sweetie," she said, turning and smiling at me.

"I'm trouble?"

"Handfuls of it," she said, giving me a knowing look and a slow nod.

I laughed.

"See?" she said, turning back to the sink full of dishwater. "You're a little troublemaker, and you like it that way. Teaching you here, with us, means you get to be you, without anyone trying to force you to be someone else. That was what we thought was the best thing for you."

I thought about this, and quietly went away, back outside and into the warming sun of a Spring day in Texas. It would get hot, soon enough. So I was enjoying the fair weather while I could.

My education didn't stop with with Gram grilling me. Gramps had plenty to teach me, too. After breakfast I'd be by his side for most of the day as we took care of something in the garden or fixed something around the house, or built something in the shed. This last was my favorite.

Gramps had given me a space of my own in the shed — my very own workbench with my own tools. He showed me how to take things apart, to be patient and find the seams and the screws, to put everything on a little tray, in the order I'd removed it, so I could find it and put everything back together again later.

He taught me how to fix small motors and large engines. He showed me how to take a watch apart, right down to the tiny gears and microscopic screws, and reassemble it perfectly — maybe even a little better. And he showed me how to troubleshoot and repair electronics of all kinds. He was forever finding old pieces of junk, thrown out by someone in town. "Just needs a little work," he'd say, smiling and dodging Gram, who disapproved of his "junk driving." They had enough junk lying about, she'd complain. But she never made him get rid of anything.

"He needs it," she told me once, exasperated and rolling her eyes. "He gets restless if he isn't building something."

Gram had her knotwork. That was her thing. She tied all kinds of knots, and just about everything had a bit of string or twine tied to it. But Gramps had his little projects. He had piles of circuit boards and bins of parts. He could take anything apart and put it back together, but most of the time it worked better when he was done than it ever had before. He could combine things — two different pieces of equipment or technology — to make something completely new.

Gram called him "a batty old engineer" once. She wouldn't explain what it meant, at the time, but I had remembered. And in all the reading I had to do, I eventually figured it out. Gramps must have worked as an engineer for a living, at some point — the kind that designed and built technology, not the kind that ran a train, which disappointed me a little, at first.

He must have retired, and so he did things to keep himself busy. But he must have been someone really smart and important once. He still was — to me and to Gram. But he was hiding for some reason. That's the impression I came away with, after years of thinking about it.

Gramps also taught me other things that had nothing to do with mechanics or electronics. He loved to go fishing and hunting and camping. He would leave the workshop behind, sometimes with a project sitting there half done, and grab his backpack and tackle. He had a "camping kit," consisting of a small tent and a sleeping roll, plus a few odds and ends for cooking on campfires. For the longest time, Gram wouldn't let me go with him on these camping trips. But at some point, around the time I turned 10, she gave in.

"You'll wear this at all times," she told me, giving me a necklace made of string. More knotwork. I rolled my eyes and she grabbed my chin, her sharp nails digging in a little. "All. Times."

"Yes'm," I said.

"And you'll sleep under this blanket every night, even if it's warm," she said, holding up one of her afghans. "Promise."

"I promise," I said.

"Even if it's just over your feet," she said, and there was a note of fret and worry in her voice.

From that point on, I constantly wore that necklace. I hardly ever took it off. It was a fine bit of knotwork, actually. Not lacy or girly, but instead tightly woven, in tiny little flourishes that looked kind of cool and unique. It rested on my collar bone, and became invisible when I was wearing a T-shirt. It was barely visible when I wore a shirt with a collar. I didn't mind it, actually. It made Gram happy. More importantly, as long as I wore it, Gram was ok with me leaving the house and wandering in the woods, or going with Gramps on these camping trips. For some reason, I never questioned why that was.

Even with her comfort level raised, however, Gram would still fret and worry each time we went. She was doing that now, as I hoisted camping gear up and into the truck, getting ready for a weekend on the banks of the Brazos River with Gramps.

She was hovering, giving advice I didn't need, cautioning me about sleeping with a blanket, keeping close to Gramps, keeping my eyes open.

"He'll be fine, Liv," Gramps said. "He's nearly seventeen! I won't let him out of my sight. I promise."

She smiled at him, and stood up and kissed him on the cheek. "I know you won't. I just wish I didn't have to go back right now."

Gramps took her shoulders in his hands, looking into her eyes. "I wish you didn't either. Can't you stay? Why does he need you there now? He hasn't been much help for the past few years."

"He has his own problems," Gram said. "But he sent me a message. He has some people he needs me to meet with, maybe offer a little safe passage. Things are getting worse. It's coming unstitched all over," she glanced at me. "He's not ready yet. It's too much."

"He'll be ready. He's a smart kid. He's going to ask me no end of questions about this conversation once we're on the road, until the fade starts kicking in."

She smiled at him, kissed him, and then hugged and kissed me, too. "You do everything your Gramps tells you, and you don't wander off."

"Yes'm," I said.

I was definitely going to wander off.

Once we got to the fish camp, all of Gram's worry and cautions were blown away like leaves in a stiff breeze. Here, next to the river, with miles of forest stretching out behind us, there was very little we ever worried about. It was one of the reasons Gramps looked forward to the trip. We could just hang out, play cards at night, fish during the day, and barely talk to each other if we didn't want to. Eventually he'd get bored and want something to tinker with, and so we'd end up heading home or going into town to do a little junk driving. But for most of a weekend, we would be here, relaxing.

I loved it, too. Especially when it was just me and Gramps.

First, Gramps wasn't quite as worried about me as Gram was. "You know the rules," he said as we unloaded his pickup. There wasn't much to unload. Gramps liked to keep it light. Whenever we saw other campers, he'd grumble that "the woods aren't a hotel," and make fun of them for their RVs and battery-powered TVs and their iPhones and iPads. We had the truck radio, and a mobile phone for emergencies. The rest was all sleeping bags and cooking pots and a moth-eaten tent patched and sewn by Gram, with a thousand bits of knotwork woven into it, of course.

I wandered away once Gramps got a fishing line in the water. He had a paperback book in one hand, its cover folded back and under. He'd have it read in an hour, despite it being a couple of inches thick. Then he'd pull another one out of from under the seat of his truck and start again. He'd be complaining about "nothing to read" by nightfall.

I moved away from the camp and out into the woods. These were technically the same woods as those running behind our house, but far enough away that everything was new and different. I had explored these woods a few hundred times, though, and knew my way well. Even if I'd never been here before, I'd know how to find my way. Gramps and Gram had taught me everything there was to know about getting around in the wilderness.

I made my way deep enough into the wood line, and I could no longer see the campground or the river. The light here, filtering through the leaves and branches above, was soft and diffused. It was light enough to see well, and I could pick my way through the underbrush with no trouble. Eventually I found the small clearing.

I'd been here before, nearly every time we went camping. The clearing was a low spot that held water during the rainy season, but dried into a leaf-covered patch of soil the rest of the year. It was open to the sky above, and ringed by great, thick trees. There were a couple of fallen trees here and there, forming benches and walls and whatever else I might imagine or need them to be. I sat on one of these now and took out a small sack lunch from my backpack. Gram had put it there, like she always did. There was something written on the sack.

"Don't get lost in those woods. Keep that necklace on. Don't forget to wake up your Gramps, and don't let him sleep next to those fishing poles all day."

Of *course* she knew. Gram always knew *everything*. I smiled and opened the sack to find a ham and cheese sandwich, a small baggie of apple slices, and a little container of peanut butter. I also had my canteen — a dented and dingy-looking metal container that Gramps had given me when we first started these camping trips. Most of the coolest stuff I owned came from Gramps. Gram just gave me knotwork and bits of string all the time.

Even now. There in the bottom of the sack was a little hand-woven patch of cloth, tucked in like a napkin. I took this out and studied it as I ate the sandwich.

I had seen these things my whole life. I couldn't remember anything from before I came to live with Gram and Gramps, but I was pretty sure I had a baby blanket made of this knotwork. I didn't own a single piece of clothing that didn't have at least one knotted pattern stitched into it, usually in the hem or under a collar, where it wouldn't be noticed. Even when I got new clothes, Gram wouldn't let me wear any of them them until they'd been washed and sewn.

I saw this so much that I had really never wondered about what it meant. It was just some little quirk of Gram's, like Gramps and his collection of parts that "might be useful someday." It had never occurred to me that there was anything *weird* about it. But as I sat there, on a log in the woods, eating a sandwich and staring at a hand-sewn napkin, I started to wonder.

What was all of this for? Why was Gram constantly tying knots, constantly sewing stitch-work patterns into everything? Why did I always have to have one on me?

I reached into my collar and pulled out the necklace Gram had given me. I'd worn it for years. She was constantly fiddling with it, like she was trying to get it just right. She would take it back, untie it, and retie it over and over. She'd add new bits of string to it, or cut some away. The length changed, from time to time, mostly as I got bigger. The pattern of knots definitely changed.

I was suddenly surprised by something I'd never realized before — I could *remember* all the knots.

I have a pretty good memory. I've always been able to recall facts, especially from stories. I could remember conversations to the last detail, and I could remember the layout of paths in the woods even after just one walk-through. My memory wasn't perfect — I sometimes forgot to do things Gram told me to do. Though she said that wasn't so much "forgetting" as "choosing to forget."

Despite a good memory, though, it was hard to believe I could remember knotwork so well. It changed so often, I would have thought it'd be impossible to remember. But I could. Every twist and loop of twine or thread I'd ever seen. Every pattern of knots I'd ever been exposed to. Every doily, every blanket, every necklace — all of it was etched in my memory.

Why hadn't I noticed that before?

I studied the necklace, and the napkin, and then I rolled up the hem of my T-shirt and studied the pattern there.

They were each different, but there were some common patterns between them.

What got me was that I could *see* the common patterns, and the differences, like they were glowing in front of me. I could see the path of each thread, and follow it from beginning to end without ever losing it. I just *knew it*. I could *feel* the pattern.

Even more surprising — I realized that I'd always been able to do this, but never really tried.

The knotwork for the necklace continued up and around the back of my neck. I pulled it around, to see where it went and what pattern it was making, but the whole thing was awkward. Finally, I pulled the the necklace up and over my head, and held it he out in front of me.

It was really complex, and it was made up of about 20 different bits of thread and twine. The pattern wove in and out, forming various shapes like hexagons and squares and even circles and curves. As I studied it, I started to pick up on a sort of "message" in the knotwork.

It wasn't like reading a sentence. There were no words. But there was *meaning*. I could see, with every twist of string, that the knotwork was telling a sort of story.

As I studied it, I got "impressions" of that story. It was a little like hearing the beat of music, muffled by a wall, but still being able to pick out the tune and identify the song. I could see, in the knotwork, a song of sorts.

It was about protection. That was a major message, repeated over and over. Protect from this, and protect from that. There was also a message about hiding. I could see that the knotwork was trying to hide something. Me, I guessed. But also something else. Not just me, but something *inside* me. Something … something …

I couldn't get to it. I could sense it like a fading dream, a memory that isn't quite ready to come to the surface. But no matter what I tried, I couldn't get under it, couldn't break through.

As I sat there, studying the knotwork and trying to figure out what it was saying, the leaves started to rustle, and branches started to sway. The wind had picked up, and the whole clearing was suddenly immersed in the sound of leaves. It was an encompassing sound, closing in on all sides, wrapping around me like a blanket. I loved that sound. It felt *safe* somehow.

Suddenly, though, the wind kicked up. A branch bent in the breeze, and swept by my face. Startled, I dropped my sandwich and the necklace.

As the necklace fell away, I saw things *shift* around me. It was subtle, but noticeable. It was like seeing a light come on through a thick curtain — like you're not quite sure if you're really seeing something or if the darkness is just playing tricks on your eyes.

I peered down at the necklace. The vague, whispering sense of its story returned, though stronger and clearer than before.

I looked around, then, at the woods and the leaves shifting in patterns of light. And I saw it.

All around me, weaving through everything, and spiraling upward to disappear into the sky, I could see the knotwork. Everywhere I looked, I could see thin, wispy threads, twisting in and out of everything, wrapping around tree branches, coiling around the log I was sitting on. Every leaf had its thin little line, connecting it to the trees, to the ground, to other leaves.

I looked back at the necklace, and the story that had been a sort of whisper before suddenly became clear.

The necklace was hiding me and protecting me. But it was also preventing me from *knowing* something — from knowing about the threads that wove all around me.

Looking at the necklace, I saw the tendrils of "string" spiraling out of it as well, forming a knotwork pattern that included me.

No, not me. I thought. My clothes.

I saw a line winding its way to the stitching Gram had put in the hem of my shirt. And that linked to stitching in my jeans, my socks, my shoes. My belt was absolutely riddled with knots. I took it off, pulling it thorough the loops of my jeans. For the first time I noticed the patterns on it, stamped deep into the leather on the inside, where it would go unnoticed. So, not just strings of knots, but any pattern of knots.

I pulled off my shirt next. Then kicked off my sneakers. The more I removed, the more clearly I could see the threads around me. It was as if, with each layer of clothing, I was unwrapping some deeper perception within me. Like tearing into a Christmas present, revealing more and more of the box inside as the paper was ripped away.

I hesitated at my pants and underwear. The last stitches of clothing on my body.

Why not? I thought, and shucked all of it. I was in the middle of the woods, by myself. The chance of anyone seeing me was pretty slim.

With the last of my clothing gone, I looked around, and my breath caught in my chest.

The thin and wispy lines I'd seen before were now rivers of golden light. They stretched in all directions, all around me, spiraling up into the sky and down into the earth. Some lines were thick, pulsing with light. Some were thin, but solid and strong. Together they all formed a knotwork, just like the knots Gram was constantly tying.

I reached out for one, and my hand passed through. But as it passed, I could *feel* the thread. On instinct, I reached again, and this time kept my hand there, in that spot.

As I watched, tiny tendrils of light branched off from it, like miniature vines. These wrapped around my arm, and when I pulled away they came with it. They hung there, insubstantial, but clinging to me.

I wasn't sure what it meant, or what I should do. I looked around, making sure no one was nearby. I looked down at my clothes on the ground, wondering if I should get dressed, go find Gramps, tell him everything. Or maybe pretend none of this had happened.

I saw the necklace.

Now it glowed. The knotwork formed points of light, like stars in a sky. And the threads that led to each of them looked like little rivers or highways, like I could step into one and go anywhere. Except the pattern of the knots was all wrong for that. I could see it. That pattern was all about *stopping*, not *going*. But if I changed the pattern . . .

I reached down and picked up the necklace. My awareness of the threads and knotwork around me dimmed a bit then, but it was too late for that. I knew the pattern now. I could see it and feel it. And as I worked the tiny knots loose, the dimness went away. So did the lit paths of the knotwork. But that was ok. I knew what the shape of it should be.

I started retying the threads and strings and bits of twine into a new pattern — much like the old pattern, but with a slightly different story. And as I worked, the tendrils of light clinging to my forearm became part of the knotwork, woven into it. Soon, I held up a new necklace — one that was part string and part light. And this necklace was built for *going places*.

I pulled it on over my head, and blinked.

The woods I'd been standing in were gone. In their place, I discovered I was standing on a mountain top, looking over a huge expanse of land in every direction.

The view was strange, like looking through one of those fish-eye lenses. It had the effect of pulling everything together, allowing me to see the full sweep of the land in front of me without having to move my head.

I could see rivers and lakes. I could see forests stretching for miles. But strangest of all, to the left and the right, stretching on for infinity, there were two huge bodies of water. It was like the land formed a barrier between two oceans — and the land stretched on *forever*, curving off into the distant horizon both ahead and behind me.

The whole scene was so strange, and so real, I found myself lost in it, staring at the infinitely long landscape. I was so engrossed in what I was seeing, I wasn't paying close attention. I stepped backward, which turned out to be a bad move. Suddenly the ground gave way under my feet, and I fell outward, into the expanse of open sky. I screamed, and on instinct reached for the first thing I saw. It happened to be one of the tendrils of light.

There was a sort of flash, and I hit the ground hard enough to knock the wind out of me. But it was soft and loamy ground, covered in leaves. The sounds of the wind rustling through the leaves once again folded over me. I was back in the woods, lying naked on the ground.

I got up and pulled on my clothes. The tendrils of light dimmed somewhat, but my knowledge of them remained. I took the napkin that had been in my lunch sack and stuffed it into my pocket. I gathered up all of my things, putting the trash away inside my backpack, just as I was taught. Carry-in, carry-out.

I took a swig from my canteen, calming myself, and then I walked out of the woods and back to the river, where Gramps was snoring next to the fishing poles, a half-read paperback making a tent over his face.

I wasn't sure what had just happened, or what it meant. But I knew who to ask, and it wasn't Gramps.

Gram had some explaining to do.

TWO | SNAGS & TANGLES

Gramps knew something was wrong, but he didn't push. He never pushed, if he could help it. He always figured I'd come around, if I were mad or scared or confused, and ask him or Gram to explain something, or help me solve something. Both of them believed in letting me work things out for myself. But some things just couldn't be "worked out."

Since discovering the threads of light, and the fact that Gram had used that knotted necklace to keep me from noticing them, a whole new world had opened up for me. Everywhere I looked, I could see how things were connected by those tendrils of light. Almost everything — especially living things — was connected. Which sounds very "Lion King, Circle of Life." But it was more than that. Things were *literally* connected, by lines of invisible energy that twisted in and around and through just about everything. In fact, when I looked close enough, I could see traces of knotwork in living things, as if the knotwork helped *form* living things. Everything had its pattern.

And it wasn't really limited to living things. Non-living things — like rocks or the metal in the truck — also had their knotwork. I just didn't see it as clearly at first, because it wasn't glowing. It was there, sort of grayed out and dim.

I did notice, though, that the knotwork created by Gram (and by me, if I counted the necklace), had that sort of "living" glow to it.

Not as bright as an actual living thing, but it was there, as if it infused and energized the string and twine.

While exploring this new perspective, I also became aware of the fact that just about everything I owned or had contact with was designed to keep me from seeing the knotwork around me. There was a repeating pattern in just about everything, but especially in everything I *wore*. I had studied it in a dozen different pieces of clothing, my blankets, my pillow, my underwear — everything had a similar pattern, telling the same story.

Hide.

Protect.

Forget.

Or maybe "forget" wasn't quite the right word. It was more like, "do not notice." And I *wouldn't* notice, unless I was looking for it. When I *did* notice, however, I felt a constant tug to forget it or ignore it.

The more this happened, the madder I got. And it happened a lot.

At first I determined I wouldn't play the game. I would refuse to sleep with that afghan, for example. Or I'd try to pull the stitching out of my shirts. Looking at it all closer, however, I discovered that the blanket wasn't part of the "forget" message, but instead talked about protecting me, and keeping me safe and hidden. My clothes had that woven into them, too. They were sending a constant message of "be safe."

So the knotwork was serving a purpose. It was functional. But it was also *beautiful*. Now that I could see the underlying network of knots and twisted threads, I could see just how much artistry went into all of it. This wasn't just some hobby Gram had, it was a *craft*. Like building fine furniture or composing a symphony. It was something she wasn't just good at, she was some kind of *virtuoso*.

But what was I? And why was she trying to make me forget it?

The truck rocked a bit as we hit every pothole in the long shale road leading away from the fishing camp. Normally this wouldn't bother me, but at the moment I had a headache. I suspected it was because I was trying hard to see the threads and knotwork around me while my clothes and the truck and just about everything else was trying to make me *not notice*. We had ridden in mostly silence since leaving the camp, and Gramps finally said, "Ok, Sawyer. I give. What did I do?"

I shook my head. "Nothing. *You* didn't do anything."

"Ah," Gramps said. "So your Gram did something. Did she put those cartoon underwear in your bag? I've told her a million times that you've outgrown that stuff."

"No," I said, but thought about it. "Well, yes. But no, that's not it. Although, yeah, I wish she'd stop treating me like a kid all the time."

Gramps chuckled. "Sawyer, I'm 63 years old, and your Gram has treated me like a kid since the day we met. You'll never outgrow her."

"Maybe," I said, sullen.

"So how is she treating you like a kid this time?" Gramps asked.

I hesitated. Maybe it was the knotwork, telling me not to reveal anything, but it suddenly occurred to me that Gramps might not know anything about all of this. And, if he didn't, maybe there was a reason for that. Maybe Gram was trying to protect him from something. I knew from reading and from TV and movies, sometimes secrets are meant to *protect* people.

Was that why Gram was keeping these things secret from me?

"Spit it out," Gramps said.

I looked at him, and then dug into the pocket of my jeans and pulled out the napkin. The knotwork in it talked about things like "freshness," like it was meant to keep my lunch from going bad. It also had other little tales woven into it, but they felt like "for good measure."

"You know the knotwork Gram does?" I asked.

Gramps looked at me sidelong. "How could I miss it?"

"Why does she do it? What's it for?"

There was a brief flash in his eyes, gone in an instant. But I caught it. I could see it still, actually. My question made a new bit of knotwork in his overall pattern. I hadn't realized I was seeing this before, but there it was. I could see some of what Gramps was thinking and feeling, evolving in tiny patches of knotwork in the pattern that seemed to be the most basic parts of him. His heart, maybe. His soul. I wasn't sure.

But one thing I *was* sure about — Gramps was getting ready to lie to me.

"What's it for?" he shook his head. "No telling, son." He laughed a bit. "You know your Gram. She has lots of hobbies. That knotwork is just one of them."

I studied him for a moment, confirming. I could see the light — twisted like a snag in his overall pattern. It didn't belong there. It wasn't true to the rest of what he knew. There was a term for that, one I'd learned in a psychology book — *cognitive dissonance*. He was saying something he didn't believe, and it was causing a snag in his knotwork.

"You're lying," I said.

He startled a bit, and the truck swerved slightly. "What did you just say to me?"

"You're lying!" I said, and I could feel a burning in my cheeks. I had never said anything like this to Gramps before. I'd never had to. It *hurt* to say it.

"Sawyer, I can see you're upset by something, but you need to be more respectful."

I started to say something then. I thought about throwing the doily at him, though that seemed kind of stupid, even a little comical. I didn't want to be either of those things right now. I wanted to be *mad*. I wanted to be taken *seriously*.

"You are lying to me" I said evenly. "You taught me that respect is a two way street, but I don't feel very respected right now."

I saw Gramps clench his jaw and grip the steering wheel harder. I saw the twists in his knotwork, too. He was mad, and I knew it. And I didn't care.

And then he relaxed. He calmed down, unclenched his jaw and his hands, and the knotwork smoothed. "Ok," he said. He slowed the truck and pulled to the side of the road. We were still pretty far from civilization, and on either side of the road were lines of trees. Barbed wire stretched along, from one stubby and weathered fence post to another, as far as I could see. I stared at those lines, and I couldn't help noticing the faint traces of light that wove in and out of them. I decided, though, that I didn't want to notice them right now. And just like that, they were gone. The world looked exactly as it should look. I glanced at Gramps, and his knotwork was invisible, too.

So I could turn it off.

"You've learned something," Gramps said. "And it must feel pretty scary right now. I know it scared me a little, when I found out about it."

I was silent for a moment, thinking about what he'd said and revealed. "So you can do it too?"

Gramps laughed, which didn't make me feel much better. But he corrected quickly, coughed a little, cleared his throat. "No, Sawyer. I can't do it. Your Gram can, though. Not me, though. I'm not like you."

I felt my face get hot again, and a pressure behind my eyes. "You're *normal*, in other words."

He laughed, sharp and loud. "Normal! Ok, well, sure. Depending on how you look at it. Sometimes I think I'm pretty below average, actually. With your Gram around, it's tough to feel 'normal.' She's a pretty remarkable woman." He trailed off a bit at the end, and I knew he was thinking about her, and maybe about to say something gross about how nice her butt was or something. I had to head that off.

"So what is it, exactly?"

He gave me a steady look. "I'm going to let your Gram explain all that. I don't know all the details anyway. I was just a dopey and slightly arrogant engineer when we met. She was the … well, that's part of the story she'll tell you. But I have to know, how did you find out? What happened?"

I thought back to the woods, and to the mountain top. I thought about the oceans and the strip of land that divided them. And I realized, I didn't really *know* what happened. It was too hard to explain. I told him what I could, about the necklace and the threads of light.

He nodded through all of it. "Ok, yep. You definitely need to talk to your Gram. And she is going to be pretty mad at me, I think."

"You? I'm the one who undid her knotwork."

He laughed. "Oh, well, that's pretty amazing by itself. She prides herself on that knotwork. She likes to brag that no one has ever been able to unknot one of hers." He gave a sharp laugh and slapped the steering wheel. "She is going to be really annoyed by that one!"

"You're pretty happy about my upcoming murder," I said, frowning.

He chuckled. "Sawyer, you have nothing to worry about. We've been expecting something like this for a long time, though we have tried really hard to keep it from coming. You have no idea."

"But I still don't understand," I said. "Why keep it from me? What does it mean? What *am* I?"

Gramps lost the smile and looked at me, his features serious, but his eyes soft. "Son, you are, right now, exactly who you're supposed to be. You're you. This … it's something your Gram is going to have to explain to you. But it's part of you, and nothing you have to be afraid of or ashamed of. Pretty much the opposite, actually."

I thought about this. "Ok. Well, I guess we'd better go face the music then."

He smiled, and laughed, then started the truck and put it in gear. "I face the music. You get a history lesson," And with that he pulled onto the shale road and we bounced our way back to the highway.

❈❈❈❈❈❈❈❈

First we had to get through all the yelling. Which, while mostly aimed at Gramps, wasn't a very comfortable experience.

"So you just let him *wander off*, no supervision, and look at what we have to deal with now!"

"We knew this was coming, Liv," Gramps said, calmly. "We'll get through it."

"I *know* we'll get through it, Drew. But he's not *ready*. He's just a boy!"

That made my face flush and my jaw clench, but I kept my mouth shut. I was almost seventeen. Legally, I could be considered an adult. But the legal system couldn't save me if Gram decided I was being smart-mouthed. I had to exercise *prudence*, as she and Gramps would say. Prudence, in the Jackson household, meant keeping your mouth shut until Gram was done yelling. She did keep a butcher knife handy, after all.

They argued, but I was suddenly feeling better. The mad was fading, and in its place was a sort of calm numbness. I felt a little sleepy. And I was starting to lose the thread of the conversation, unable to remember exactly why Gram was "gettin' her ire up," as she'd say.

Thread? I thought.

I shook my head, then focused on seeing the threads of light and the knotwork around me. And because I *wanted* to see it, I *did* see it. Everywhere. Everything in the room had bright patches of knotwork. The walls were covered in it. If I thought the doilies and dreamcatchers and braids were all over the place, those were just tiny threads in a much larger tapestry. *Everything* in our house was part of a larger knotwork.

And at that moment, while Gram was yelling at Gramps, I could see things shifting. Everything in the house funneled into one large thread, about the thickness of my wrist, that looped and coiled but ultimately ran straight to Gram.

I could see that as she got her ire up, the network of light around me was changing slightly, responding to her. It was sending a new message, or broadcasting one of its many messages much "louder."

Forget. Do not notice. Sleep and forget.

"Stop it!" I said, standing from the soft chair. I'd been settling into it without even realizing it, about to doze. About to forget.

Gram and Gramps stopped and stared at me. Gram's mouth was still slightly open, and her eyes were still a touch wild, but softened as she looked at me.

"Sawyer," she said, and suddenly her voice was calm. Gramps slid in beside her, put his arm around her waist, which made me even more mad, for some reason. "Sweetie, I'm sorry. It's automatic. I know you can sense it now."

"What's he sensing?" Gramps asked.

She looked up at him. "The *forget*. The house knows I'm upset, so it's trying to calm me down by making him forget." She looked at me then. "But that's not going to work now, is it?"

I was still mad, and still ready to get my *own* ire up. But I took a breath, calmed myself, and said, "No."

She nodded, and then, as I was watching the knotwork of the house, she made an adjustment. She reached out and grabbed a braid of string that was on one of the side tables by the sofa, and in a quick motion she un-knotted it. Hanging there, loose, I could see that even though it still had its connection to the larger knotwork of the house, that connection was wispy and tentative. Whatever energy flowed through the knotwork still clung to it, in part, but it was a little like watching water drain from a balloon. The energy was starting to dwindle and shrink, fading into a thin thread.

Before it was gone completely, however, Gram was tying. In quick movements, she braided the string again, twisting in small coils and loops as she went. She was incredibly fast, and as I watched I could see that wispy bit of energy start to grow brighter. When she was done, she held up the braid. It was a different pattern than before. The message had changed.

"This charm will help," she said, and handed me the braid. "Attach it to your necklace."

I reached into my shirt and took out the necklace. I used the loose bit of string at the top of the "charm" she'd just made, and tied it to the the middle cluster of knots in the necklace. As I did this, I saw the energy of the home connect to me, just like it was connected to Gram. A thick rope of energy formed, coiling its way deeper into the house. I was a part of the knotwork of the house now.

Gram stepped forward and peered at my necklace. "You've changed this," she said, inspecting it closely. Then she looked up at me, her eyes wide. "I can't read it," she said.

"What do you mean?" Gramps said from behind her, peering over her shoulder. "How's that possible?"

She shook her head. "It shouldn't be. But then, there's never been a *Teth* like Sawyer before."

"A what?" I asked.

She looked at me then, and I could see a bit of sadness in her eyes. Whatever she was about to tell me, she'd wanted to protect me from it. I wasn't sure if I knew that from her expression, or just because I knew her so well. Or maybe I was picking it up from her knotwork, which I could see shifting and twisting in small knots and tangles. Some of the tangles were coming loose. By now I recognized that as a sign that she was about to come clean on a few lies. Not all of them, I noted. But if she wanted to keep some secrets, how could I blame her?

"The *Teth*. As in 'tether.' It's a very old word here. Even older where we come from."

"Where do we come from?" I asked quietly.

She sighed, and I saw even more of the tangles and snags loosen. "A place called the Long Land. It's one of the Layers — one of the deepest, actually."

I started to ask what the Layers were, but she held up a hand. "There's a lot of this, Sawyer. There's so much you just don't know yet. I'll get to all of it, I promise. But you're going to have to let me tell it in my own way."

I closed my mouth and nodded.

"Good," she said, then turned and looked at Gramps.

"Three coffees," he said, nodding and walking into the kitchen. They were always doing that. Gram almost never had to ask Gramps for anything. He just *knew*.

"Is Gramps a *Teth*, too?"

Gram burst out laughing, sharp and loud.

"I heard that!" Gramps said from the kitchen.

Gram reached up and wiped a tear from her eye, still laughing a little. "No, Sawyer. Your Gramps isn't a *Teth*. I'm sorry, this isn't going to make much sense, but it's an old story and a very old joke. Let's just say there's some history around the idea of your Gramps as a *Teth*, and we'll get to that some other time."

I nodded. "Ok."

"So, to start … well, the *Teth* are a culture of people from the Long Land. Not really a race, but more like a bloodline. There are a few branches. Some of the *Teth* went their own way, thousands of years ago. They stepped into the Layers and were never seen again. Or so people thought. Turns out they were up to all kinds of things in the Layers."

I didn't understand any of her references, to layers or *Teth* or the Long Land. But as she talked, I started getting "impressions" of it all. It was like a memory, but not one of my own. Instead it seemed to come from all around me. I looked around and saw that as Gram talked, the whole house glowed gently. I could feel a warmth growing inside of me. It was comforting. Not like before. The house wasn't trying to make me forget. In fact, it was trying to make me remember something that I'd never actually experienced.

The house — the knotwork that wove through everything, including me and Gram — was telling me a story as Gram spoke.

"The *Teth* are a bloodline that goes back to the beginning of time," Gram said. "The real beginning of time, not just time for this Layer."

"What do you mean by 'layer?'" I asked.

"Don't interrupt, sweetie, it will make this take forever."

Gramps came in with three steaming cups of coffee. Gram and Gramps took theirs black, and normally I would pour in cream and sugar until what was left resembled syrup more than coffee. But I was feeling a little grown up and the moment, with Gram and Gramps talking to me so directly. And I was feeling a little defiant, too. I had this sense that there were a lot of expectations already on me, that I didn't even know about. So I took my cup and sipped the black brew, trying not to wince from the heat or the strong flavor, and doubly trying to ignore the arched eyebrows and exchanged smirks between Gramps and Gram.

"The Layers," Gram continued, "are what our people call all the different realities. Remember the rock face we saw in Austin, when we were on the lake that time?"

I nodded.

"That lake was man-made, and as they cut away at that rock face they revealed the strata. Gramps went on and on about sediment and geology."

"We call it 'education' on this Layer, sweetie," Gramps said.

She smacked his bicep with the back of her hand, never taking her eyes off of me. "The Layers are kind of like that, only each stratum is a universe, or a different reality. If you go down deep enough, you'll find the very first Layer. The Long Land."

I thought about this. Layers upon layers of reality. I'd read about this sort of thing in books about physics, but more often in science fiction. "Alternate realities?"

"Parallel, mostly," Gram said. "Though your Gramps did introduce me to alternates. Mostly when we say 'Layers,' we're talking about *parallel* universes."

"Different multi-verses," Gramps said. "Different Bubbles."

"You and your 'Bubbles,'" she said, shaking her head. "That's not going to catch on."

He smiled, tight-lipped, and nodded, "We'll see."

Gram turned back to me, "That's a whole other story, again. There are as many stories as there are Layers, I bet. But we're only talking about *this* 'Bubble' for now," she said, shooting Gramps a look. "For the most part, the Layers all operate by the same rules and physical laws. Gravity is pretty much the same from one Layer to another. Energy is still energy. The laws of thermodynamics are the same."

She glanced at Gramps when she said this last part, and he nodded without even looking her way. He was lost in thought himself, and I got the impression that he, too, was "hearing" the story as it wove its way through the knotwork of the house.

I watched it as it grew. A light pulsed and brightened among the threads, and as we went on we became more and more entangled in it. Gram and Gramps glowed brighter as the story unfolded, and I could tell that it was very personal to them.

I looked at my hands, but couldn't see that there was any of that brightness there. Maybe I wasn't close enough to the story yet. I could see the threads starting to wind and knot around me, though.

"If you go deep enough in the Layers, you will eventually come to the Long Land. Our people, the *Teth*, have called that Layer home since time began. We believe it's the very first Layer, the oldest, because no matter where you go from there, no Layer is older. We have ways of checking. And since it's been thousands of years since the *Teth* first started walking the Layers, we're pretty confident we would have found an older Layer by now."

"Assuming it still exists," Gramps said.

"Don't start that again," Gram said, shooting him a warning look.

"I'm sorry, I thought we were telling the *whole* story," he said, shrugging in that way we both knew would get him a smack, eventually.

She shook her head instead. "This is confusing enough, I'm guessing." She looked at me. "I know you must have hundreds of questions, but just wait, and listen, and let's see if they're answered."

I nodded. She was right. I wanted to ask so many questions, I was practically on fire with them.

"The *Teth*, our people, were born with the ability to see and manipulate the knotwork. You've noticed it by now. The threads of light that seem to connect everything."

"Yes," I said, and was on the verge of firing off dozens of questions when she held up a hand.

"The knotwork is just one way of seeing the binding energy of the Layers. We see it as pattens, like bits of twine or rope wound together in loops and knots and kinks. The *Teth* are born with the ability to read the patterns. We can tell when someone's lying, for example."

"When you see the snags!" I said, unable to contain myself.

She smiled lightly, nodding. "Yes. Good, you've picked up on that," she shot Gramps a look.

"Yeah, yeah. The jig is up, then," he said.

"We knew we wouldn't be able to lie to him forever."

I was torn between the feeling of elation that Gram was confirming what I knew about the snags, and the feeling of hurt over discovering they had been actively lying to me. One tempered the other, and I settled somewhere in the middle, waiting.

"So all *Teth* can see the knotwork. And, with practice, all *Teth* can manipulate it by tying knotwork patterns made of string or twine or anything that we can tie a knot into, really. In fact, it's the pattern, not the material that matters. We can do the same by drawing a pattern on a piece of paper, for example, or in the dirt."

"Or stamping it into the leather of a belt?" I asked.

She peered at me. "Spotted that one, did ya?"

I said nothing.

"Yes. Anything, really. The knotwork isn't as strong when it's tied to a drawing or a stamp or something, though. I believe it has an affinity for string and rope and twine. It seems to like it."

"You're not going to tell him the knotwork is *alive*, are you? Our only evidence of that is anecdotal at best, and I haven't even managed to …"

"Hush!" she said, punching his arm. "Who's telling this story?"

Gramps waved it off, and Gram continued.

"Once a *Teth* has a pattern that tells the story they're trying to tell, they can infuse it with the energy of the knotwork. The quality of the pattern will determine how strong the connection is. The more intricate the pattern, the more powerful it can be. The knotwork is so complex, no one can get to the core of it. We've tried for millennia. But some of us have gotten pretty good at weaving stories of our own into the knotwork.

"What you really need to know, Sawyer, is that when the *Teth* create a pattern, and energize it with the power of the knotwork, they're creating a new *reality* of sorts. They're 'dictating localized reality,' as your Gramps would say." She glanced at him and he nodded.

"Tell him about the wizards," Gramps said, smirking.

She shot him a dirty look.

He shrugged. "It's part of the story."

She sighed, and rolled her eyes. With a shrug she said, "Well, he's right. Thousands of years ago, some of the *Teth* discovered that if they created the right pattern, they could step into the knotwork and move into new Layers. Some, who were particularly gifted, could use the knotwork to do incredible things. There are tales of *Teth* who could create objects out of thin air, or even turn one object into another, just by changing their local reality. Doing things such as this is incredibly difficult, and more than a little dangerous. The knotwork doesn't like it when you change the pattern too drastically, especially if it's against the will of whatever or whoever is being changed. It causes knits all over the place. And those knits can cause tears in the fabric of the Layers."

"And then Xander has to come along and fix and stitch the tears, which gets him all weird and grumpy," Gramps said.

"He doesn't *know* about Xander yet, you doofus," Gram said.

Gramps looked me square in the eye. "He's coming, don't you worry," Gramps said. "And when he shows up, watch your Gram. She becomes a school girl. All 'Oooh, Xander, you're *so* clever!'"

Gram elbowed him harder than usual in the ribs, and he grunted, rubbing his side as he winced.

I could see, in the knotwork, a weird sort of twist in the air. There was something about this Xander guy that really did get under their skin. Gramps was clearly jealous of him. And Gram … well, as I learned to read the the knotwork more clearly, I could see something in her when his name was mentioned. It was something similar to the knotwork that wove its way between her and Gramps. Was that love? I was too new at this to be able to tell, and part of me was afraid of what it would mean if it was.

"Xander is a story all his own," Gram said. "The point is, the *Teth* can sometimes manipulate the local knotwork in ways that some people might consider … well …"

"Magic," Gramps said, smiling.

"Not *magic!*" Gram said. "It just *looks* like that!"

Gramps held his hands up in an *"ok, ok"* gesture.

I was hung up on what I'd just heard. "Wait … what does this mean, exactly? If it's not magic, what is it?"

"It's science, just like you're used to," Gram said. "Just science that most people don't understand yet. The *Teth* have a natural affinity for seeing and working with the knotwork, but it's about like someone having an affinity for playing music or repairing a car engine. Anyone could learn to do it. Some are just naturally better at it than others."

"I'm terrible at it," Gramps said.

"Yes, Dear. Everyone knows that," Gram said, patting him on the knee.

"Thought I was pretty good at it once, though," Gramps said, dreamily. "Had a machine and everything."

"We don't need to hear about the machine right now."

"It was a beauty," Gramps said.

Gram rolled her eyes. "In the past, whenever a particularly talented *Teth* found his or her way into the Layers, they would sometimes use their abilities to make a name for themselves. Here, in this Layer, several clusters of *Teth* spent an awful lot of time going around being hailed as wizards and worshiped as gods. Merlin and Mordrid. Zeus, Odin, Set, Quetzcoatl, Vishnu — pretty much all the gods of any pantheon you've ever read about."

I blinked. "Wait … those gods were *real?*"

"And huge jerks, mostly," Gramps said.

"You've *met them?*" I asked.

"Not all of them," Gramps admitted. "Some of them are dead. Some are trapped in the knotwork*oof!*"

Gram elbowed him hard in the solar plexus, and Gramps immediately coughed and sputtered and cursed a little.

"My story, *my* timing," Gram said.

Gramps nodded, winded.

"Sawyer, sweetie, this is all a bit much to handle in one chunk. So I'm going to give you something." She stood and left the room, walking to the back of the house. When she came back a minute or so later, she had a braid. Unlike the others that were all over the house, all over everything, this one looked *old*. Entwined with it, I could see bright tendrils of light, spiraling and coiling outward, connecting to the house and the larger knotwork in thousands of places. It was also connected to Gram and Gramps. There were tangles and knots between them and the braid that I couldn't quite read, no matter how hard I tried.

"This is probably the oldest braid in the history of the Layers," Gram said, quietly. "My mother gave it to me. It belonged to your mother, for a time. And now I'm giving it to you."

At the mention of my mother, I became even more intrigued. We didn't talk about her much, except wistful stories about her growing up, about her and my dad being good parents, about how much she loved me. Never anything about where she went, or what happened to her. I used to ask, when I was little. Now I hardly ever thought to, for some reason.

I took the braid cautiously, afraid it might unravel or fall to pieces. Anything so old had to be fragile.

Instead, as soon as I touched it I could feel the *strength* of it. It felt more substantial and real than anything I'd ever felt before. I looked up at Gram, and she was smiling.

"You feel it," she said, beaming.

"What is it?" I whispered.

"Everything," Gram said. "Everything I know, anyway. And everything my mother knew, and her father, and his grandfather, and on and on. All the way back to the earliest days of the *Teth*. You're holding the entire history of our people."

I marveled at it, watching the folds of the knotwork — the threads of light — weaving in and out of it. As I watched, the story started to unfold. I saw the *Teth,* and their first steps into the Layers. I saw the ancient *Teth* who placed themselves above humanity as gods. I saw *Teth* who roamed the Layers, fixing the damage done by those who abused their power.

"Xander Travel," I said. The name just popped into my head.

Gram was nodding, and Gramps rolled his eyes.

I watched, through a sort of daydreaming, as the man calling himself Xander Travel moved from Layer to Layer, fixing the tears and rips caused by the *Teth*. I saw him untangle the snags, using odds and ends like kitchen utensils and odd-shaped stones and shirt buttons. Lots of shirt buttons.

"Is he a *Teth*?" I asked, confused. "He's doing something different."

"It's the buttons, right?" Gramps asked, and Gram elbowed him again.

"Yeah. Lots of them," I said.

"That's sort of his thing," Gram said. "And no, he's not at *Teth*. He's an Exemplar."

"A what?" I asked.

"The first ones. The model humans, used by Layers as the template for human life. Xander is the last of them."

I blinked. "You're telling me he's … what … the *ultimate* human?"

"He likes to think so," Gramps said, and he was up and dodging before Gram could hit him. "Your Gram thinks so, too!" he said, ducking as she flung a TV remote at him.

"He's an old family friend, and that's it!" Gram said.

Gramps ducked back into the kitchen, laughing. But as I watched the knotwork, I could see that he really was a little jealous of Xander. There was history there, and it involved some heartache and pain.

"Where is he? What happened to him?" I asked.

"Out there," Gram waved to the distance. "Moving around in the Layers. Him and that 8-Ball of his. Don't even ask. But there's more to the story, Sawyer. A lot more. Keep that braid. Tie it in with your necklace. And when you get time, study it, daydream with it. You'll eventually get a pretty good idea of our history."

I took off the necklace, and without even thinking about it I knotted the braid into it. By this point, I expected the necklace to be bulky, hanging weird. But instead, it was like a tight winding of heavy-gauge string, with a small network of knots in the center. I could see past the string itself, into the knotwork of it, and all the complexity within. The braid had just become a seamless part of it, disappearing into it. The knotwork, though, was bright and complex and I could stare at it all day.

"You're very good at that," Gram said. "Much better than I was when I was your age. It's a little frightening. I've never seen anyone take to the knotwork so easily."

"I don't even know how I do it," I said.

She smiled. "No, I expect you wouldn't. But you'll learn. The braid will help. And your Gramps and I can get you started."

I nodded. "So is the history lesson over?" I asked.

"Almost," Gram said. "The thing you have to remember, about being a *Teth*, is that you not only have an ability, you have a responsibility to use it wisely. So many *Teth* ignored that responsibility, or flat-out turned their backs on it. One in particular decided to use his abilities to rule. It took a great army to bind him to one of the Layers, to contain him." She became quiet, and I could see sadness wash over her. "It cost us a great deal," she said.

I felt her sadness, but couldn't help being fascinated. "Who was it?" I asked.

"Aeodymus," she said.

Gramps came back into the room, this time with a plate of cookies.

He set this on the coffee table between them, and snagged one to dip into his coffee. I did the same.

"I've heard that name before," I said around a bite of chocolate chip cookie. "When the Ink attacked." I said this as if the memory were as clear as the morning, but it wasn't. It had only been in the past day or so that I even remembered that attack, years ago, when I hid in the shed while Gram took care of the Ink.

She nodded. "I blocked that memory from you for a long time, but it doesn't surprise me that it's back."

"Why?" I asked, though I wasn't sure which "why" I meant. *Why did you block my memory? Why did it come back? Why me?*

Gram shook her head. "It's difficult, Sawyer. What you know can influence the knotwork. It can be a Tell. That's a knot that can be read from far away, under the right conditions. Every knot we make in the knotwork pulls at some bit of it elsewhere. So if you want to know when someone utters a phrase or has a thought, you can set up a Tell that triggers when one of those things happens. It's like a loose knot that pulls free. Aeodymus actually has one tied to his name. I've blocked it from here. You can block a Tell by creating slack, by tying a knot of your own to the name."

"I … see …" I did not see. All of this was making my head swim.

"Don't worry, kid," Gramps said. "She's just getting started. She'll explain this a few times in a few different ways, and suddenly it will be clear." He smiled at her, and instead of punching him she smiled back.

"So Aeodymus is a *Teth*. And he used his power to do something bad. And to punish him, the *Teth* imprisoned him on one of the Layers."

Gram nodded. "See? Getting it already."

"Why doesn't he just leave?"

"He can't. Xander and the other *Teth* bound up his knotwork in that Layer in such a way that if he tries to leave he could come completely unraveled. And that's not pretty. He's been working on it for about a ten thousand years, though," Gram said.

"Ten thousand! How old is he?"

She shrugged. "Maybe thirty? It doesn't matter."

"Are the *Teth* immortal? Am *I* immortal?" That was an interesting thought.

Gram laughed. "No, sweetie. Not even close. Aeodymus can die, and so can you. But there are ways for the *Teth* to live extended lives. Moving around in the Layers can sort of reset the clock, in a way. Aeodymus has figured out a way to prolong his life, even while stuck in one layer. However he's doing that, it allowed Xander and the others to trap him. He's bound with the fabric of the Layer. At the time, he was pretty sure he'd figured out a way to achieve his goals," she shuddered. "Though why he'd want to, only he can know. And he *did* figure a way. Thankfully he can never leave that Layer."

"So we're safe from him," I said.

"Not even close," Gramps said. "Those Inks of his are like his personal army. They scour the Layers on his behalf, looking for anything he can use. They slip through tears and open weaves."

Gram nodded. "They're like vermin. Dangerous vermin."

A thought occurred to me. "And they're looking for me."

Gram and Gramps avoided glancing at each other, but I could see the knotwork move, like a pre-echo of movement. "Why?" I asked.

Gram sighed loudly, and grabbed one of the cookies. She took a bite, chewed, and looked off into the distance. When she swallowed she said, "If he can get his hands on you, he can be free. And he can pretty much become god of all creation."

I choked on my coffee, spitting it out in a spray. Gram and Gramps both cried out, and Gram grabbed one of the doilies on an end table and used it to dab and dry coffee from everywhere. "Honestly!" Gram said. "Who does an actual *spit take*?"

"Sorry," I said. "I guess there was something about me being the key to godhood that went down the wrong pipe."

Gramps chuckled. "It's a lot to take in, I bet."

"Yeah," I said.

"Well, it's nothing to worry over too much. You're safe here. I've done everything I can to keep you 'off the radar.' The Inks occasionally pick up a scent, but we can hold them off, and hide you all over again."

I thought about this. "But I can't hide forever. Eventually, I have to leave here."

They looked at each other.

"Right?" I asked.

"I think we should tell him," Gramps said.

"Well *now* we have to," she said. She turned back to me. "You can't leave here, Sawyer. Not really. You can go out for short trips, like camping on the river, or vacations to Austin or Disney World or whatever. Occasionally. But being out in the world, outside the protection of the house, it makes you vulnerable. No matter how well I try to hide you, the Inks will eventually zero in on you. It's too risky. The only way to keep you safe is to keep you here, on this Layer, on this property."

I took this in. "So, I'm as much a prisoner as Aeodymus," I said, quietly.

"No," Gram said, shaking her head. She stood and then knelt beside me, putting her hands on mine. "No, sweetie, never. You're not a prisoner. It's just … it's the only way to keep you safe and keep Aeodymus from escaping."

I thought about this, and about what it meant. Stuck here, forever. There seemed to be plenty of room for me to roam. I was apparently allowed to go deep into the woods, all the way to the river, even on family vacations. But always with my grandparents. Always with knotwork everywhere.

A thought occurred to me.

"Gram, what does the Long Land look like?"

She looked wistful. "Well, depending on where you are, it can look like just about any type of setting. There are cities and forests and mountains. All the things you'd expect to see on any world, really."

"Are there oceans?"

She and Gramps exchanged looks again. "Yes," she said cautiously. "Two of them."

"And they're separated by a long strip of land? Oceans on either side?"

"How did you …" she started, and then stood. "Oh no," she said.

"What happened?" Gramps asked.

"He piggybacked!"

"What? How? I thought that was impossible, with all the knots you have all over him!"

"The necklace," she said, nodding my direction.

It was still out, hanging over the collar of my T-shirt.

"He retied it," she said. "And there must have been a stray thread, from when I went over. He retied it without even thinking about it, and accidentally stepped through to the Long Land!"

I felt my heart pounding. "What does that mean?" I asked. "What did I do?"

"It means we have to get out of here," Gram said. She turned to Gramps. "He's not safe here anymore!"

THREE | ON THE RUN

The truck rattled and jostled out of the driveway, bouncing in the familiar potholes harder than I was used to. I was strapped into one of the seats in the extended cab, along with three hastily packed bags. Gramps was driving and Gram was …

Well, mostly Gram was yelling.

"Faster! We have to get far away from here!" She was fiddling with a spool of twine she'd grabbed before leaving the garage. I watched as she formed a complex pattern, and the knotwork spoke to me, talking about hiding and protection. The knotwork spread out from the twine, covering us in a net. It folded into the knotwork laced throughout the truck, adding to it. Tendrils of it reached into each of us, and I saw how our pattern became a part of the knotwork weaving through our surroundings.

"What's happening?" I finally asked. "What did I do?"

Gram turned in her seat and looked at me. "You did what comes naturally, Sawyer. It's ok."

"That place I saw — that was the Long Land?"

"Yes," she said.

"How did I get there? One minute I was in the woods by the river, eating my lunch. The next I was standing on a mountain."

"It was the knotwork in your necklace," she said, nodding to my chest.

I pulled the necklace out, looking at it as best I could, dipping my chin so I could see.

The necklace had the braid in it now, so the story it was telling was *huge*. It was like flipping through the pages of an entire set of encyclopedias. Like endlessly clicking on Wikipedia entries.

"Should he be messing with it?" Gramps said, peering at me through the rearview mirror.

"He's fine," Gram said. "You know how this works."

"Well he accidentally jumped Layers before," Gramps replied.

"That's more my fault than anything," Gram said, looking at me with concern on her face. "I should never have kept all of this from you for so long, Sawyer. You deserved to know. Most *Teth* learn about jumping Layers when they're very little. I thought maybe we wouldn't have to, since you didn't know anything about the Layers or the Long Land. I was a fool."

"How did I do it?" I asked. "What if it happens again?"

She shook her head. "It won't, unless you want it to. And you might, before it's all over. But it happened because I was careless. I was asked to go back to the Long Land, to meet with Xander and some of the other *Teth*. Usually, when you jump between Layers, you tie off your entrance. I left it open, in case I needed to jump back suddenly."

"Why would you need to do that?" I asked.

She gave me a strange look. "For you, sweetie. If you were in trouble, I would jump back to help. The knotwork in your necklace would tell me. I attached a thread from my own knotwork. It connects us no matter where we are, even across Layers. That's why it happened, though."

"Liv," Gramps said, shaking his head. "After everything we've been through." There was a note in his voice, like he thought it was kind of funny.

"Shut up," Gram said. "This is different."

He chuckled.

"So you left an opening, and because we were connected by a thread, I jumped to the Long Land? What was keeping that from happening anyway?"

"You retied the knotwork," she said, and she smiled. "No one else could have done that. Not one of *my* knots, anyway."

"She's proud of you right now," Gramps said, "but she's going to complain about this to no end later."

She shot him a look, but I could tell, by now, that they were bantering more for my benefit than out of any real annoyance with each other. Ever since this started, they'd been picking at each other. But their knotwork told a story of deep love and dependence.

Gram looked at me again. "When you retied the knotwork, you added something in. You energized it. You took up some of the slack in the line. And with the gateway open between this Layer and the Long Land, the knotwork just pulled you through. Not quite to my location, apparently."

"I was on a mountain, and then I fell."

"Fell?" she said, her eyes wide.

"Yeah, and suddenly I was back in the woods. I was …" I hesitated.

"You were what?" Gram asked.

I felt my face go flush. "I was naked."

Gramps laughed, loud and sharp, and Gram put a hand over her mouth, stifling a giggle. "Why?" she asked.

"The knotwork in my clothes was keeping me from seeing everything … look, I had no idea about any of this, ok?" I felt myself getting embarrassed, and then angry.

Gram must have sensed it, because she made an effort to bring herself under control. Gramps made no such effort, and chuckled as he drove. The dark road stretched out beyond the headlights of the truck, and I could see walls of trees on either side. My whole life I'd lived near these woods, and for the first time they seemed frightening to me. Normally, the woods made me feel free. Now, though, rumbling away in the dark, running from monsters that were out to grab me, all these trees made me feel trapped.

"Why are we running?" I asked.

Again Gram and Gramps traded looks. "The Inks know where you are now," she said.

"The Inks? Those oily black monster things? How?"

"When you went through to the Long Land, with no knotwork to hide you, it's pretty likely you triggered a Tell. Maybe more of a Snare, though not a binding one. It's a small knotwork, triggered by a Tell. It snags you. Some are designed to hold you in place, either physically or just on a Layer. That's more or less how Xander has Aeodymus tied up. He can move around on his Layer all he wants, but the Snare keeps him there."

"But I was able to come back," I said.

"It may be a non-binding Snare. It grabs hold, but it doesn't keep you in any one place. Instead it works a bit like a tracking beacon. It follows you everywhere. Speaking of which ..." She stared at me, hard, looking me up and down. She was looking at my knotwork, the personal knotwork that was part of who I was. After a moment, she said, "There it is. I can't believe I didn't spot it before. But it's smaller than a Tick!"

"Can you remove it?" Gramps said. "Are we hidden from it?"

"Not by much," Gram said. "And yes, I can remove it. Give me a minute."

She reached out and grabbed ... *something*. It was the knotwork, I knew, but I couldn't see it. But I did *feel* it.

As she tugged, it was like feeling a cord tighten around my stomach. The more she pulled the tighter it got.

"It hurts!" I said, doubling over.

She put a hand on my shoulder, straightening me back up. "I know, sweetie. Just a moment longer." She tugged some more, brought her other hand down and started working on the invisible knot. The tightness increased until I thought I'd be cut in half. I struggled just to breathe. Then, suddenly and mercifully, I felt a sort of release, and I could breathe easier again.

I looked and saw that she was holding a glowing thread between her fingers. I doubted there was anything there in the "real world." But I could see it well enough. "It's just a thread," I said, still huffing a little.

"It is now," Gram said. "It was a Snare a few seconds ago. It looked like this." She did a few quick twists and loops, pulled at the thread in a few places and then held it up dangling from one hand.

I looked at it closely. The pattern was simple enough, once I studied it.

"Think you could make one, if you had to?" she asked.

"I'm not even sure how this works," I said.

"You're a natural at it," she said. "Once you've seen a knot, you can make it from memory. As long as you understand the story it tells."

I nodded. "I think I can make this."

"Good," she said, then rolled down her window and tossed it out. "They're tracking that, I'm sure," she said. "When it disappeared, I'm sure they noticed. Now that it's back, they may suspect what I'm doing. But just in case."

"I couldn't even see it, when it was on me," I said.

"No, it was telling you that it wasn't there. You'll have to be on guard for changes in your knotwork, especially if you're going to move around in the Layers."

I thought about this. I'd learned so much over the past few hours, and not all of it made much sense. I looked at my own knotwork, as best I could. I could see definite patterns. I looked at Gram and Gramps, and saw their patterns, too. All three were complex and impossible. And they were constantly shifting, changing slightly with every second. How could I possibly keep track of any changes to my knotwork? The whole thing was *constantly* changing!

Except …

I saw now, the difference between my pattern and the pattern of knotwork from outside. The bits of string and thread woven into my clothes, with little stories of protection and hiding, were *different* than my knotwork. They were infused with light, but not in the way I was. My light was pulsing and living. The light was changing in rhythm to my knotwork, whereas it was static and unchanging in the patterns woven into my clothes.

All I had to do was look for anything that wasn't changing *with* me.

"I can see you figuring it out," Gram beamed. She was twisted in her seat, hands on the headrest and her chin on her hands.

"Yeah," I said. "It's weird."

Gramps grunted. "Just wait. Weird comes from all over."

Gram rolled her eyes. "He's just jealous. He doesn't see the knotwork, just its effects. Unless he's wearing the goggles."

"Goggles?" I asked.

"I made them myself," Gramps said, puffing up his chest and talking in his fake "pride" voice. "Just a little science and engineering genius, that's all."

Again Gram rolled her eyes, but this time she leaned over and kissed him on the cheek. "Yes, dear. You're the smartest man in all the Layers."

"'Cept for Xander Travel," he said in half-kidding pity.

"Oh, let's not start *that* again," she said, smiling.

Suddenly something dropped hard onto the hood of the truck.

Gramps cursed and slammed the breaks. Tires squealed and ground over the blacktop as we slid to a halt. Gram was jarred in her seatbelt, and twisted back to face front, her left hand folding around her waist to hold her ribs on the right side. "Ink!" she yelled.

I saw it. Big and black and oily. It crouched on the hood of the truck, looking at us through the windshield, snarling.

"He dented the hood!" Gramps said.

"We've got *bigger problems*, Drew!" From somewhere I didn't see, Gram drew out her butcher knife. As I looked at it, though, I could see it wasn't a butcher knife after all, but was instead some kind of short sword, with a bell-shaped guard at the hilt. Woven into the metal, from pommel to hilt to blade, was an intricately engraved knotwork that told all kinds of stories. It spoke of concealment and camouflage, but it also told a story of cutting and slicing, of piercing armor and splintering bone. This was a sword forged for a real warrior.

And it belonged to Gram.

She had the door open and was out facing down the Ink in seconds. Gramps tugged at his seatbelt a couple of times before finally getting it to unclick, and then he was out the door. I was out next.

"Get back in the truck!" Gram yelled.

"Not a chance," Gramps said. He was hefting a tire iron. Just a regular tire iron, from what I could see.

"You're just going to split his attention. I need him focused on me!"

Sure enough, the Ink turned from Gram, the sword-wielding warrior, and faced Gramps, the tire-iron-wielding grandpa.

This wasn't going to be good.

It occurred to me, that Gramps was the only one standing between me and the Ink, and that the Ink was actually after me. It would tear through Gramps to get to me, I knew.

What did I have? No weapons. Not even a tire iron. Just the clothes on my back and …

And the Swiss Army knife.

I pulled it out of the watch pocket of my jeans and opened the blade.

It wasn't a sword, but it did have an awful lot of knotwork tied to it. Though, somehow, the knots looked weird, even a little clumsy. And most of them were tied back to Gramps.

He made this, I realized. *Even with no natural ability, he somehow made this*. It wasn't the first time I realized how smart my Gramps was, and how inventive, but it did make me feel suddenly much closer to him.

The knotwork in the knife told all kinds of stories, not just one. It had multiple functions, multiple uses. It was a Swiss Army knife, after all. I smiled, and then rushed to stand side-by-side with Gramps. I held the knife in front of me, the blade pointing at the Ink as menacingly as I could manage.

"Idiots!" Gram shouted, and then she rushed forward, leapt up onto the bumper of the truck, and then its hood, before flying toward the Ink, sword raised.

It saw her at the last moment, and raised an arm in defense.

The blade of her sword sliced through the Ink's arm almost as if it weren't there. The creature howled, and it sounded like someone dragging dozens of heavy metal objects across a concrete floor.

Gramps ran forward then and took a big swing at the thing's head, clobbering it good. The Ink's head spun to one side, but it quickly recovered and backhanded Gramps, sending him flying into the ditch on the other side of the road.

I yelled, and was just about to rush forward and do a bit of stabbing when Gram yelled back. "Go check on him! Leave this thing to me!"

I halted and looked at her, a bit dazed, and then turned and ran for Gramps.

I found him in the ditch, groaning and rubbing his chest. The tire iron was nowhere to be seen.

"Lost m'tire-iron," he mumbled.

"I see that. Gram is pretty mad at you, I think."

He managed to get to his knees and then stand. "She's been mad at me as long as I can remember. Nearly killed me when we first met."

"You'll have to tell me the whole story when we get out of here," I said.

We hobbled back to the truck, where Gram was exchanging feints and thrusts with the one-armed ink. Despite its handicap, it didn't lack in dexterity or viciousness. Every swipe of its clawed hand came a little too close to Gram for my taste.

"Stay back!" she said, without even looking at us. "I mean it."

"Staying back," Gramps said, holding up a hand in mock surrender.

The Ink snarled and swiped again at Gram, but then tried to leap to the side and make a dash to us. She headed it off. "Get Sawyer into the truck!" she said.

Gramps took me by the arm, but I shook it loose. "Sawyer," he said, sternly.

But I wasn't listening. Not to him.

I was listening to the knotwork.

The Ink wasn't right. It had a knotwork of its own, but the story didn't quite fit. In fact, it somehow seemed *obscene*. It was a twisting in the knotwork — life created by mutilating the natural pattern. And woven throughout was a sort of dark and disgusting looking version of the knotwork. It made me feel slightly nauseated.

Was this what Aeodymus could do? Create this ugly, vicious life? And worse — by doing so, he was creating a snag in the knotwork. A lie. But a *living* lie, which somehow made it worse.

I could see all of this, even as Gramps tugged at my arm and Gram fought off the thing that was trying to get me.

I stepped away from Gramps.

"Sawyer!" he shouted, grabbing at me again.

I kept moving, kept pulling away. He was injured, and all his strength was going to just keeping himself upright. I was fine. More fine than he or Gram realized.

As Gram fought the thing back, it noticed I was close, and tried even harder to get to me. I had no doubt that if Gram weren't there, it could snag me and have me in another Layer before I could say anything about it. But with her distracting it, and with it injured, I saw I had a chance to do something.

I could *unwrite* the story.

It took a swipe at me, and Gram parried. I ducked under her arm, ignoring her shouts and screams, and dove directly into the midsection of the Ink.

It was taken by surprise, and I had just enough momentum to make it stumble backward. Before it could reach me, however, I shoved my hand into it.

No, not into *it*. Into its *knotwork*.

I grabbed a cluster of threads at its heart, felt the energy of the knotwork pulsing through it, felt how the rest of reality hated this oily black creature. I had its heart — its true heart, the essence of what it was — in my hand.

I tugged.

It didn't take much. One tug did most of the work. The bit of actual knotwork it was tied to was actively repelling it, trying to be free of it but held firm by the dark knotwork.

The Ink stopped moving, and instead started howling. It was a high and mournful yowl, like all the pain in the universe was being funneled through this thing. I ignored it, and now with both hands I was working at the knotwork of it, untying it, cutting some with the Swiss Army knife, letting the threads drop loose.

I stood back just as the entire knotwork collapsed in on itself. As I did, my view of the Ink changed, and I could see the creature itself now. The knotwork that kept it "alive" was gone, and the body of the thing now liquified and oozed like a puddle of oily goo. In moments, it was completely dissolved, a black stain on a blacktop road in the middle of the night.

"What did you do?" Gram whispered.

I was huffing and trying to catch my breath, staring at the spot where the Ink had been only seconds before. "I untied it," I said.

I turned to look at her and saw her standing with the sword hanging at her side. There was an odd look on her face — one I didn't quite recognize. A mixture of awe, and maybe a little disgust. I wasn't sure. Had I done something wrong?

"There are more of them," Gramps said suddenly, pointing. We looked and saw them.

Dozens. Maybe more. A small army of Inks was shambling down the darkened road, caught occasionally in the headlights of the truck.

"We have to leave," Gram said. And with that she reached into her blouse and pulled out a knotted necklace of her own. She grabbed my arm, and then Gramps put a hand on her shoulder. With a quick gesture, as if tying a small bow, Gram opened a gateway just in front of us, and we all stepped through, leaving the road, the truck and, most importantly, the Inks, behind.

We were in the Layers now.

FOUR | THE LAYERS

The first time I left my own Layer, it was by accident. The switch from home to the Long Land happened so quickly, I really didn't know what happened. This time, as Gram guided me and Gramps through the gateway she'd opened, I could see it all.

For starters, it didn't really look like a "gateway" as much as a gap in a weave of fabric. It was as if someone had picked apart a piece of cloth, opening a gap wide enough that three human beings could walk through. And as Gram closed the gate behind us, I saw that what she was doing was a little like pulling threads to cinch and close a bag. The gap became smaller, the threads curled and twisted off into their original pattern, and suddenly we were no longer where we had started.

Though, at first glance, I might not have been able to confirm that.

"We're on a road in the woods," I said.

"Good observation skills, Robert Frost," Gramps said, chuckling. He was rubbing his shoulder, where the Ink had hit him. Gram was also rubbing her side. They'd both taken a pretty bad beating. All because of me.

"I'm sorry about this," I said.

"Sorry about what?" Gram asked. She wiped the blade of the sword on the grass at the side of the road, getting it as clean as she could. Now that she wasn't using it, I could see the camouflage re-exert itself, hiding the sword as a butcher knife.

"I'm sorry for getting us into this mess. Going to the Long Land. Getting caught by the snare."

"Did you do it on purpose?" Gram asked, peering at me.

"No!" I said, a little too loudly.

Gram smiled. "Then it's not your fault, is it Sawyer?"

I shook my head. "No," I said again, quietly.

"He doesn't believe it," Gramps said. "He's definitely his mother's son. Always taking responsibility for everything."

At the mention of my mother I perked up, hoping to hear more. I'd lived with Gram and Gramps for as long as I could remember, and had no memory of my parents at all. They never volunteered anything, and for some reason I never asked.

Did Gram make me forget?

I decided that if she did, she must have her reasons. I wanted to know about my parents — desperately. But I suspected I'd know in time. "I think we need to get moving," I said.

Gramps chuckled. "Yep, just like his mother. He's already picking up the 'vibe.'"

"Hush you old fool," Gram hissed. She turned to me, "Don't listen to him. But as for us being on a road in the woods, you're seeing the similarities between here and where we were, right?"

I nodded.

"Remember how I told you about parallel realities? Well, some of them actually are *alternate* realities. This one is in the Layer next to Earth Prime."

"Earth Prime?" I asked.

She blinked, shook her head, then gave Gramps a sour look. He was grinning wide. "Now you have *me* doing it."

"It's catchy," Gramps shrugged.

Gram rolled her eyes. "That's the name your Gramps gave it, because it's the Layer he came from. He thinks of it as zero, or the midpoint on some kind of chart he has in his head. He's numbered all the Layers he's been to in order, as near as he can."

"There are also lettered clusters, and letter-number pairs that ..." Gramps said.

"Not now!" Gram said.

Gramps chuckled, and then stepped off of the road. He found a tree and started breaking off branches, then took out his own pocket knife and started cutting and trimming away the smaller branches from these.

As he did this, Gram took a seat and watched. I sat beside her. I wasn't sure what else to do.

"Don't help or anything," Gramps said. "I got this."

"Just want to make sure you don't feel left out," Gram said.

I started to stand, to go and help, but Gram put a hand on my arm. "Sit," she said. "I want to talk about what happened back there."

I sat. "Ok," I said. "But to be honest, I'm not entirely sure what that was."

"You did something ... Sawyer, you did something that is just plain scary. You didn't just kill that Ink, you *unraveled* it. Somehow you reached into its knotwork and cut away the core. I've never seen anyone do that before."

I didn't know quite what to say, so I said nothing. Instead I picked at the grass on the side of the blacktop road. It was dark, but there was just enough moonlight to show some details. Once off the road, the world dropped into complete darkness. That frightened me a little, knowing that the Inks could be out there, hiding.

"Will the Inks find us here?" I asked.

"Eventually. But they have no idea which way we went, and there are billions of directions to choose from. Chances are pretty slim they'll be able to track us down right away. They were only able to find us on ... *Earth Prime*," she shuddered and Gramps let out a loud *ha!* from the tree line, "because they knew we were there, somewhere. Aeodymus has had them scouring the place. I thought they'd eventually give up, since we were pretty well hidden. But if Aeodymus has learned anything in his thousands of years of imprisonment, it's patience."

"So why did we stay on Earth Prime, if we could have run to any of the Layers any time?"

Gram shook her head. "Too dangerous. Well, maybe it was *just* as dangerous. But at least, staying in one place, we could give you a stable home to grow up in. On the run, that's no life for a child. Besides, Xander told us Earth Prime was the safest place for you. 8-Ball told him that."

"Who is 8-Ball?" I asked.

It was Gramps who answered. "That annoying little floating ball of ..."

"8-Ball is just about the only thing your Gramps and Xander have in common," Gram interrupted, before Gramps got too colorful.

"Not counting you, of course," Gramps said.

"Oh, you irritating old man, you *won* didn't you? I chose *you*. And I've never regretted a minute of it. Until right now!"

They bantered, and the love glowed, bright and steady. This was something they'd done all my life, and I knew, instinctively, that it was their way. But now, with the ability to see the knotwork and the connection between them, I could see that it was a much more powerful bond than I ever could have expected. They weren't just in love, they were *bound* to each other. They were tied together so tightly, one couldn't exist without the other. I hadn't seen the knotwork for any other couples, but I was betting that what Gram and Gramps had was something unique. It just looked and *felt* unique.

Gram turned back to me, "When you reached into the Ink, what was going through your mind?"

I shook my head, then shrugged. "I can't say for sure. I saw you squaring off with it, and then I saw its knotwork. There was this cluster in the middle. It was ... I don't even know how to describe it. *Obscene* I guess. It was like seeing an ugly patch on a nice suit, but worse. Because the patch was sort of alive, and it had nothing *good* in it. It was just evil. Pure evil."

Gram nodded. "You did something unbelievable. And ... well, I don't know if you can do that to anything other than an Ink, but I'm going to ask you never to do that to a human being. No matter how foul or evil they may be, they don't deserve that. It's ... it's like *unmaking* them. Like taking their story and ..."

"And unwriting it," I said. "Yeah, that's what I was thinking, just before. I could unwrite it. I could take its story away."

Gram looked at me, hard, then nodded.

"I won't do that to anyone," I promised. "I understand."

Again she nodded, saying nothing.

Gramps came back to us then, carrying three long branches. He had cut off all of the smaller branches, and sharpened the ends to make them into spears.

"What's that for?" Gram asked.

"Weapons!" Gramps said, incredulous.

"What do we need *those* for?" she asked.

"Did you not see me making these the whole time? You could have told me not to bother any time."

"I have a *sword* Drew," she said, holding up the sword in question.

"That butcher knife?" Gramps said.

She blinked. "You know good and well that this is a sword in disguise."

They went on like that for a while, as we stood and started limping down the road. Despite the seeming objections from Gram, I was actually grateful for my spear. Having any kind of weapon felt right, at the moment. Gram pointed out that if we ran into anyone — humans, at least — they might not appreciate our need for spears and butcher knives. She put the "knife" into her belt, and as far as anyone could tell it disappeared completely. I could see it, though, and for what it was. She had a scabbard on her belt, which I had never noticed before. Gram, it seemed, was a master of hiding things using the knotwork. I studied what she'd done, and then stopped and picked up a long stem of grass from the side of the road. As they watched, I twisted this into a small series of knots, along with some of the glowing knotwork around me, just as I'd done with my necklace, back in the woods. I tied this around the shaft of my spear, and as I did so the knotwork of the spear became part of the pattern. I watched the twists and knots and loops come to life, in a sense. I wondered, then, why it would be necessary to create the pattern using string or twine or grass. Why not just manipulate the knotwork directly?

"Whoa," Gramps said. "Did you just make your spear invisible?"

"He did," Gram beamed.

I did the same for the spear Gramps was carrying, and included a twist of my own. I linked a thread from Gramps to the spear, with the story that he could see it at all times. Again, Gram approved, complimenting me on my natural skill. Gramps hefted the spear and nodded, pleased. And, with that done, we were on our way.

With all the talk of "Layers" and other worlds, I wasn't sure exactly what I was expecting on our first day in an alternate universe.

I was hoping for at least something *different*. Instead, we sat in a restaurant that was identical to one we went to on Earth Prime (Gram still hated the phrase), and we had a meal that was identical to what we usually ate.

"Shouldn't there be flying cars or people with two heads or something?"

"Oh! R-1238. That one had people with two heads," Gramps said.

"Don't even pretend like you have every universe memorized," Gram said, shaking her head but smiling.

"Only the interesting ones. And not even all of those. There are quite a lot of them." He ate another forkful of pancakes, looking dreamily off into the distance.

Gram shook her head, but the trace of her smile stuck around. She looked at me. "The *alternate* realities are tricky. And usually boring. Just about anything can trigger a replicating pattern in the knotwork. It's a bit like fractals. You know what fractals are?"

I knew the word, thought about it for a second, and said, "They're from geometry. Repeating patterns. I know they use them for modeling things in computer graphics, like snowflakes or trees."

She nodded. "A fractal is a curve, like a spiral. Every part of it is characteristically the same, varying in position and orientation. No matter how closely you look at a fractal, it will resemble the larger whole."

"So every universe is a fractal of a larger universe?"

Gramps interrupted, "You realize there's a whole bunch of math that goes with fractals, and you have an engineer sitting right here at the table?"

"We're not doing math right now, we're doing theoretical and hypothetical construction," Gram snapped back.

"In other words 'making stuff up,'" Gramps huffed.

"It's a *metaphor*, you nerd."

Gramps stuck his tongue out at her and both Gram and I burst out laughing.

After a moment, Gram shook her head and started again. "The important bits to remember are that every *alternate* universe is more or less the same as the one next to it, with tiny little differences. Sometimes so tiny, they would seem insignificant. They may never even be discovered. And every alternate reality is part of a cluster that your Gramps calls a 'bubble.' Rational people call it a *multiverse*," she shot Gramps a side-eyed look, which he ignored in favor of putting more syrup on his pancakes. "And the multiverse is part of an even bigger cluster he calls the *omniverse*."

"Omni means 'all encompassing,'" Gramps said, smiling.

"You're a doofus," Gram said. Gramps chuckled and wiggled his eyebrows at us as he drank his water and crunched on an ice cube.

"Ok, I think I get it," I said. "So that covers alternate realities. What makes a parallel reality, then?"

"*Dippernt multiberse*," Gramps mumbled around the cube of ice.

I blinked. "Huh?"

"Different multiverse," Gram said, and she dipped her fingers into her glass of water before flicking them at Gramps.

I thought about this. "Ok, I get it. Clusters of alternate universes make up a multiverse. Parallel to each multiverse is another multiverse, and within that is a cluster of its own alternate universes. So those are parallel but not alternate to our own."

"The kid gets a prize!" Gramps said, raising his glass in a mock toast.

Gram smiled. "He was always the smartest man in the house."

"Hey!"

She laughed and slid closer to him, throwing her arms around his shoulders and kissing him on the cheek. "You were never in the house much," she said.

Gramps grumbled and said something under his breath, but it was all good natured. I found myself smiling, too. It was a relief, to be in this moment. It felt right. It was almost as if everything that happened last night hadn't happened after all. We were all tired, a little dirty, and a bit banged up, but otherwise this was your typical day on Earth Prime.

A thought occurred to me.

"Can the Inks track me now?" I asked.

Gram shook her head. "No, not without the snare. And I'm on the lookout for any now. They can't lace the entire omniverse with them. We might come across one randomly, but I wove in a bit of protection from them. A sort of early warning system with a slipknot."

"So all of us are protected?"

"Well, you are," Gramps said. "Those things don't actually care much about me, unless I get in their way. And they generally try to avoid your Gram. It's the only sign of intelligence in them that I've seen."

Gram patted him on the cheek for that.

"About that," I said. "You're a sword-wielding, demon-slaying granny?"

"She knows Kung Fu, too," Gramps said.

"I do *not* know Kung Fu. The *Teth* train in different martial arts."

"But …" I said, picking up the butter knife from beside my plate and swishing it around like a sword.

"Put that down!" Gram said, smacking my hand.

I laughed a little and put it down.

"Your Gram isn't an ordinary *Teth* either," Gramps said. "She's a Bloodline Guardian."

"It's just a title," Gram said, demurring.

"A sight better title than 'engineer.' I constantly have to explain to people that I don't drive a train."

I laughed, which is never a good idea with Gramps, who takes it as encouragement.

Before he could break into a routine that would attract a lot of attention, Gram interrupted. "I trained my whole life to protect the bloodline, to prepare for the day when you would arrive," she said.

"Why me?" I asked.

Her face became serious, and she leaned forward slightly, hands on the table, looking at me intently. "The knotwork tells a story, Sawyer. We can't know all of it, that would be impossible. But the *Teth* have studied their part in it for eons. Long ago, we discovered that something was going to happen. A big event, so evil and so destructive, it could cause the entire knotwork to unravel. The *Teth* immediately started preparing, creating twists and knots that the next generation would pick up and tie and retie. The pattern eventually became complex enough that it evolved on its own, and carried through into the Layers. That pattern was the start. You're the result."

I stared into the glass of water in front of me, watching the condensation trickle down its outside and pool on the paper table cloth, spreading wider and wider in its *own* fractal pattern. "So, I'm just some bit of knotwork, made to do a job?" I asked.

Gram reached out and grabbed my hand, squeezing hard. "No. You're so much more than that. In a way, we're all just knotwork, when it comes down to it. But you — no one *made* you, they just started the wheels turning and *prayed* you'd appear before we needed you. And now, here you are."

"But you were keeping me hidden. You were going to keep me on Earth Prime forever," I said.

"Yes," Gram said. "Xander told me to do that. He told me that would keep you safe. The *Teth* hoped for you, but we hoped even more that we wouldn't *need* you."

"Well, that's nice," I said. "It's everyone's dream to grow up and be *not* needed."

I meant it as a joke, but it fell flat from my lips. It was the first time I realized I actually meant what I was saying. It was the first time I felt any sort of bitterness or resentment about my life, or toward these two people who had been parents to me for as long as I could remember.

To my surprise, Gramps stood and came around the table. He pulled my chair out and away, with me clinging to it and looking at him, wide-eyed. And then he reached down and more or less picked me up into a hug, rubbing the back of my head with one hand while squeezing my rib cage in the other.

I struggled a little, but ultimately just let it happen. Gramps was never much of a "hugger." Neither was I. But I knew — I could always tell, even before I could see the knotwork — that emotions could run deep for him.

"You have always been needed," He said into my shoulder, squeezing so hard I thought some ribs might pop.

He let me go then, and walked away, toward the restrooms.

I sat again, and tried to be sly about wiping tears from my eyes, masking that I was suddenly crying.

"Oh, you and your Gramps. You're both idiots. You think it bothers anyone that you're crying?"

"It bothers me," I said.

"Him too," she said, shaking her head. "He's the smartest man I've ever known. If you tell him I said so, I'll stab you. But smart as he is, he's just plain dumb when it comes to expressing how he really feels. It was almost a deal breaker, when we first fell in love. He jokes, you might have noticed."

"It may have occurred to me," I said.

"And you're just like him, sometimes. Jokes, to cover what you're feeling, to control what people think of you. It's a very basic form of manipulating the knotwork. It rides right on the edge of creating a kink, like a lie would. But it's safe. And he's a good man," she said, looking off to where he'd gone. "Once I realized he wasn't a liar, and I no longer wanted to kill him, it didn't take long to fall in love with him."

I thought about all of that, and what it meant. Gramps was a good man, that was true. Gram was good, too. They were both smart, and both strong. I had to ask.

"Am I a good man?"

Gram looked at me, and her expression softened. "Sawyer, you're definitely a good man. You never have to worry about that. You're also the one who gets to decide what you do with your life. Don't ever think that you're not. We were hiding you, it's true. But we always knew that at some point you'd know all of this, and you'd make decisions that we couldn't control. We just wanted to keep you safe for as long as possible, and to give you the kind of home that would make you the good man you are today."

I thought about this, wiping the pesky tears away again, taking a sip from my water. It helped. I felt calmer. I felt better, and less bitter.

Because she was right.

I didn't know exactly what I would do, but I did know that I would have to start making decisions for myself. Because even though I loved and trusted Gram and Gramps, they had, in fact, lied to me my whole life. They had covered the truth, and used the knotwork to keep me ignorant.

I loved them. I forgave them. I would never let them or anyone else have that kind of power over me again.

Gramps came back from the men's room. "We'd better get moving. We can't stay here too long."

A thought occurred to me. "Will we run into alternative versions of ourselves?"

Gram shook her head. "Not a chance. There is no alternate version of you anywhere in the knotwork. You may be the only unique person to ever live."

That was interesting. It made me pause for a second, thinking of what that could mean. It gave me a sort of thrill, hearing it. "What about you and Gramps?" I asked.

"This multiverse isn't the one I came from. There's very little chance of an alternate version of me here."

"And I live in a big city somewhere, in pretty much every universe in this cluster," Gramps said.

This shocked me. "You? In the *city*?"

"Oh, *that's* surprising? Well I wasn't always all fishing and tinkering in the garden, Sawyer. I was a research engineer, and a good one. People paid me a lot of money to design and build things. And I liked being close to where the technology was."

"What changed?" I asked.

He glanced quickly at Gram. "I built something that took me into the Layers. I met some amazing people. I went on some interesting and terrifying adventures. And I fell in love with the most stubborn but amazing woman in the Omniverse."

"You mean me, right?" Gram asked, a fake look of confusion on her face.

He smiled, leaned in and kissed her solid on the lips. "I'll never mean anyone else."

They were getting mushy on a level that made me want to gag, so I pushed ahead. "So where do we go? If you don't live around here, is our house still here? Could we hide out at the fish camp?"

"Oh, he doesn't mean we need to leave this restaurant," Gram said. "He means we need to leave this *multiverse*. We can't go gallivanting around in this cluster. We'll eventually be noticed. There's nothing dangerous about meeting your alternate self, usually, but your Gramps went and made himself rich and famous everywhere. He's going to get noticed."

I boggled. "*Gramps?* Rich and famous?"

"Hey!" Gramps said. "Don't sound so incredulous. I was kind of a big deal, in my day, before I hopped universes. I used to hang out with Wozniak and Sergey Brin and all the really smart rich guys. I had my own tech company. *I usedta be somebody!*" He said this last part in a fake sort of Bronx voice, which made me think he might be quoting a movie or something.

"Yes, dear," Gram said, standing and patting his shoulder. "You were the next Steven Gates."

"*Bill* Gates. Or Steve Jobs. You know the difference!"

Gram turned to me. "Are you ready?" she asked.

I stood, and snagged the two invisible spears leaning against the wall near our table. I handed one to Gramps, and held the other one upright, puffing out my chest a little, trying to be the epitome of cool. "Let's go," I said, in what I hoped was a "great hunter" kind of voice.

Gram rolled her eyes. Gramps chucked my chin and dropped some cash on the table to cover the bill. We walked out of the restaurant into the hot and humid Texas air, where Gram twisted open a gateway. I studied it, seeing how it was made. The knotwork was amazing, and beautiful, and maybe a little scary.

I took one last look around. This place wasn't *home*, but it sure looked like it. And this might be the last time I ever saw it. I inhaled deeply, trying to fill my lungs with the place, to make it part of me as much as possible, before stepping through the gate and into the Omniverse.

FIVE | HELLO, XANDER TRAVEL

By now I was getting used to looking at the world in terms of the knotwork. I could see the patterns of it spiraling and twisting everywhere. Sometimes it was like a spider's web — a thin and almost invisible net of gossamer threads that I really couldn't see until I got up close. At other times, it was like a tapestry, looking solid and substantial when you were standing away from it, but revealing all of the fine detail and craftsmanship when you got up close.

And like a tapestry, the knotwork had its story to tell. It wasn't a static and frozen scene, but was constantly shifting and changing and evolving.

Back "home," in the multiverse that contained Earth Prime, the pattern was more or less "familiar" to me. The story was something I understood, almost without trying. I could never know all of it — there were too many paths to follow and too many threads to study. But I got the general sense of it, by instinct.

Here, I felt suddenly *overwhelmed* by the story.

I gasped as Gram closed the gate behind us, and fell to my knees.

Gram was there in an instant. "It's ok, it's ok," she said.

"It's so *much*," I said, feeling like I was drowning. And, in a way, I was. I was drowning in stories. I was drowning in the pattern of the knotwork. This place, wherever it was, had a *thickness* to it. It was like trying to drink a glass of molasses before taking a breath. It flowed over me, through me, threatening to wash me away, or absorb me into it.

"Breathe," Gram said. "Just concentrate on breathing. Listen to my voice. Look at me. Do you see my thread? The main thread, the line that connects me to you?"

I looked, and I did see it. How could I see it? There were so many! So many threads, weaving in and out of her, in and out of *everything*.

"Follow that thread, Sawyer. Just the one. Focus on that thread. Come to me."

I tried, but kept getting sidetracked. I'd follow, and then a branch would form, a tangent would entangle me. "Just that thread, Sawyer. Just that one thick thread that connects us. Follow that one."

I did. It was difficult, but it started to ease. And as it did, Gram became my entire focus, and the rest started to fall away. Eventually, though it felt like forever, all I could see was Gram, and the knotwork pattern that was the *her* of her.

I was huffing, breathing like I'd just been running. My head throbbed a little, and my heart was racing. I felt sick to my stomach, and I breathed deep until it passed. I calmed. I felt better.

"Good," Gram said, stroking my face, clasping my hand. "Good. You're good. I'm sorry, I should have warned you. I forgot what it's like, the first time."

"What happened?" I asked.

"You were overwhelmed by the knotwork. We just stepped into the Long Land. It's at the heart of the knotwork for the whole Omniverse. You were trying to read the story of all of creation, all at once. It's enough to tear someone into pieces."

My breathing slowed, and I was able to get to my feet, a little shakily. I hadn't even realized I was on the ground. "I don't understand. I've been to the Long Land once before, on that mountain. This didn't happen that time."

"No," she said. "You were still under the influence of my concealment knotwork, more or less. Sort of like a numbing agent. There were still tendrils of it clinging to you, even though you were … well, naked in the woods for some reason." I started to explain, embarrassed, and she waved me off. "It was keeping you from really seeing the knotwork clearly. But now, you're wide open. You haven't had much experience with this, yet. You're a natural with all of this, but even you need some training. We'll work on that."

I looked at her and Gramps, and then around at this place we had escaped to.

"The Long Land," I said. Cautiously, slowly, I opened myself up to looking at the knotwork, seeing the pattern again, this time in small sips. It was just as immense and dense as it had been before, but it wasn't overwhelming me. It was like I'd been dunked into an ocean when we first got here, and I panicked and tried to swim. Or, maybe, I tried to *drink* the ocean. Now, it was more like tackling a rather large glass of water. Maybe more than I can handle, maybe too much to take in all at once, but I could take sips instead of gulps.

"You'll have to develop the habit of turning down your ability to see the knotwork, when you travel. It will eventually become automatic. You can keep looking, keep seeing and reading the story of where you are and who you're with. Just don't run with the channel wide open all the time. It's easy to ignore all the input when you're standing in the middle of it, but when you move from one cluster to another you'll be flooded."

"Got it," I said. I felt much better, actually. And a little antsy. We were in a brand new place. What little traveling we did, back on Earth Prime, everything seemed more or less "normal" there. Here, however, the whole world had a new flavor. Everything felt energized and alive, in a way I had never noticed back home.

"This place always feels like I'm getting a full-body shave," Gramps groused.

"Hush, you love it here," Gram said.

"Loved. Past tense. Before I was beaten to bread dough and nearly executed."

"We cleared all that up," Gram said, waving him off.

We were standing on a hill of our own, high enough to give me a sense of the place. I could see stands of trees in the distance, a forest that was more or less like the woods I grew up in. Except ... *more*. I couldn't quite figure it out, but it seemed like I wasn't looking at just *any* forest. I was looking at *the* forest. As if I was seeing the model upon which all forests were built.

"Everything here seems so ... *ultimate,*" I said.

Gram laughed a little. "The Long Land is the home of the Exemplars. The *Teth* come from here, but we suspect we didn't start here."

Gramps spoke up, "This place is more or less what Plato had in mind when he wrote about *ontos*. It means 'ideal.' It was his philosophy that somewhere in creation there was a level of reality that was the basis for everything we know and experience. If you had a chair, somewhere there was an 'ultimate' chair, the model of 'chairness,' and that ultimate would have all the perfect characteristics of what makes a chair a chair."

"And that's where we are? Ontos?"

"That's what I called it when I discovered it," Gramps said, grinning.

"You did not discover the Long Land, you old fool!" Gram said. "It *always* existed."

"Yeah, but I was the first person from Earth Prime to find it. So I discovered it. And I get to name it."

"Name it anything you want," Gram said, rolling her eyes. "The rest of reality will keep calling it by its proper name."

She turned back to me. "Are you feeling well enough to travel?"

"Yeah," I said. "Where are we going?"

"To a cabin a few hills over. It's hidden in the woods. We can wait there until he comes."

I blinked. "Until *who* comes?" I asked.

She smiled and looked at Gramps. "Xander Travel is on his way."

Gramps stiffened, and cursed under his breath. "Fantastic," he said, and started marching off toward the hills.

Gram and I followed, and as he tromped ahead, I stepped in close to her and whispered, "Why does Gramps hate this Xander guy so much?"

"He doesn't," she said. "He loves him. It's kind of impossible not to. But he's a little … *jealous* of Xander. There was a time when I wouldn't give your Gramps a second look, if you can believe it."

"Because you were in love with Xander?" I asked.

She nodded. "I thought I wanted to spend the rest of my life with him, even though he'd outlive me by a very long stretch. Even if I kept manipulating my knotwork, like the wizards, and kept myself alive indefinitely, Xander would eventually outlive me. Or outgrow me. He's a wonderful man, but he's alone. Terribly alone. Even with others surrounding him. It was one of the things that drew me to him. He could stand in a crowded room, with all eyes on him, with everyone rapt by his every word, and he would still be the loneliest man in the Omni."

"Why is he so lonely?" I asked.

"He's the last of his kind. The last Exemplar. He might have left the Omni long ago, and let the knotwork be whatever it was going to be, if it weren't for the unraveling. Or, I guess, if it weren't for the *Teth*."

I absorbed this, thinking, mulling over the meaning of it. "If the *Teth* have caused so many problems, why doesn't he want to wipe them out or something? Sounds like he could do it."

"He could," she nodded. "I believe that. If he felt it was necessary to keep the Omni protected. But he never will. He's a good man. The model of good men, actually. He doesn't see the knotwork the way we do, but he knows it exists. The *Teth* have their place in the Omni, even when we sometimes foul things up. Xander has sworn to protect the Omni. He's the only one left who can, in his estimate. It's his burden to bear."

I thought about this as we walked. Gramps, up ahead of us, still seemed in a huff. I could see tendrils spiraling off of him, fading to nothing. I was starting to recognize things like this. I could see the emotions at play in Gramps, ideas forming that went nowhere. He was imagining or remembering, and it was fueled by his emotions. Anger, maybe. A little. But also a sort of fear.

"Gramps is afraid he'll lose you," I said.

Gram looked at me, surprised. "Oh? Why do you say that?"

I nodded toward him. "I can see it in his knotwork."

She peered at him, then looked back at me, wide-eyed. "You can see that? What he's feeling?"

I didn't know what to say. "Can't you?"

She shook her head. "What else can you see?"

I shook my head. "I'm not really sure. I see a lot. I only just pieced together what I was seeing in Gramps, just now. I can sort of read emotions. A little anyway."

"And thoughts?" she asked.

I shook my head. "No, not really. Not that I've noticed."

She nodded. "You are amazing, there's no doubt. I've never met a *Teth* who could read emotions. I've heard it was possible. The wizards could do something similar, twisting the knotwork of a crowd to get them to be angry or afraid or whatever was needed. Some could control minds, make people into puppets. All of these things cause knits, though. So please, be careful. You want to avoid tearing the knotwork, trust me."

"Ok," I said. Then, thinking about it, "Is his name really Xander Travel?"

She laughed. "Well, yes. It's the name he chose for himself. The 'Travel' part is more like a description. It's what he *does*, more than who he is. He travels the Omni, fixing the tears, fighting back the things that leak through from one Layer to another. I told him, once, that he should rename himself 'Xander Protector.' He nearly threw up from laughing."

"Why? Sounds pretty appropriate."

"Maybe," she said. "But he doesn't see it that way. He's protecting people. Protecting all of reality. But he sees that as more a responsibility, and not really his to choose. He's … well, he's *honored* to do the work. Tired. Lonely. But honored."

"I can't wait to meet him," I said.

Gram said nothing, and we walked on.

About an hour later Gramps stopped and waited for us to catch up. He was calmer now, back to being practical and reasonable. "I think this is it, right?"

Gram smiled. "Yes. Not bad."

Gramps shrugged. "I've learned a few tricks since the first time."

"Well, from here I'll take point," Gram said. "I'll have to turn off the snares and drops."

Gramps turned to me. "As she walks into those woods, you stay directly behind her, ok? And directly in front of me."

"Ok," I said.

Gram stepped off the road and crossed to the woods. She walked up to two trees standing close together, forming a sort of "V." I watched as she manipulated a bit of knotwork, and suddenly a gate — a fence gate, not one of the knotwork gates — appeared out of nowhere. It had been so well hidden, even I couldn't see it. She opened this and walked through. I followed, reaching out a hand to hold the gate open as I passed through. There was a tension to it that told me there was a spring in there to pull it closed, along with any snares or traps attached to it. Gramps followed behind me, and I heard the gate clack shut. I glanced back just in time to see it disappear, replaced by an opening that led to the road. I was pretty sure that we were now on a path that didn't really exist in those woods, and that no one could see or hear us from outside.

We were on a stone path that ran straight as an arrow through the woods. Trees lined it on either side. Though, as I looked, I notice that sometimes the trees weren't so much *lining* the path as growing over it. And, at one point, I could swear that we were actually walking *through* a tree.

"*This* is weirder than I'm used to," I said quietly.

Gramps spoke up from behind, his voice at normal volume, which sounded unreasonably loud and startling to me. "It's fine. We're sort of in a tunnel. Your bloodline made it a long time ago. It's a weave of knotwork that opens a space between universes."

I looked closer at my surroundings. Sure enough, there was a tightly woven bit of knotwork forming a tunnel over us. I started to step closer, to get a better look, but Gramps reached out and grabbed my shoulder, hard.

"I told you to stay directly behind Gram," he said.

I nodded. "Yeah, sorry. What happens if I step off of the path?"

"Not sure," Gramps said. "But it's not a tangle I want to deal with at the moment."

Again I nodded, and we walked on.

The path seemed to stretch forever into the darkened forest. Unlike the woods back home, here I didn't feel quite so snug and comfortable. On the path, there were no forest sounds, no feeling of a breeze, no insects buzzing or chirping. It wasn't exactly *silent*, it's just that the noises were *wrong*. It was like hearing a freeway in the distance, or the sounds of a party on the other side of a thick wall.

"So we're *between* universes?" I asked out loud, not bothering with whispering this time.

Gram answered, "Yes. Though don't ask me which Layer is on top of us. I'm pretty sure it changes."

"I think the whole system rotates, like an orbit," Gramps said. "I haven't been able to study it, but I've thought about it for a long time."

"Yes," Gram said. "I know." She then broke into the voice she used whenever she was imitating Gramps. "'Do you think a new universe rotates into position? How about orbital decay? Do you think they'd let me put some instruments in the tunnel?' I've heard these questions for forty years."

"Kill a man for being curious," Gramps grumbled.

"I almost did once. Don't tempt me!"

I smiled. The banter was a welcome change to plodding on in silence, and it made me feel a little more at ease. I think that being in the forest without actually being *in* the forest was probably the first time the weirdness of the Layers really hit me. Or maybe it was just the energy in the air, here in the Long Land. Something had me feeling a little strange, anyway. And with everything that had happened so far, this trek through the tunnel was making me jumpy.

Finally, after what seemed like miles of walking in dense twilight, I started to see a soft glow of brighter daylight up ahead. After a while, I could see open sky in patches above us. Not long after that we came out of the forest into a large, circular clearing. There was another fence gate here, and Gram worked the knotwork and the locks, opening it so we could walk through and into the glade beyond.

The glade was huge, and as far as I could tell it was perfectly round. I could see other fence gates along its perimeter, and hundreds of stone paths leading like branches to a main trunk — a cobble stone road that cut through the center of the glade and led directly to a large, wooden structure in the middle.

"*That's* the cabin?" I said, my jaw hanging.

The structure was *enormous* — larger than any mansion I'd ever seen. It rose high into the sky, in multiple stories of stacked logs and support beams. Windows, with actual glass, dotted it from floor to roof, along with balconies made of twisted tree branches and vines.

It was a log cabin, alright. But it wasn't like any log cabin I'd ever seen on television or in books. It was far more than a stack of hewn logs, crisscrossed together to form walls. It seemed more like a *living* thing. It was composed of trees and branches that still had their natural shape, and yet every piece fit together perfectly.

The base of the cabin was either constructed of or surrounded by large stones. A porch extended around the entirety of it, as far as I could tell, and this was shingled in tree bark and bright green leaves.

I looked at it in the knotwork and saw that it was bright with activity, telling a story of safe harbor, comfort, rest, recovery. It said everything but "welcome." In fact, laced throughout its knotwork was a warning to stay away, if your intention was to cause trouble.

"It's more like an inn than a cabin," Gramps said, putting a hand on my shoulder. "She's a beauty."

"She's one of the oldest structures in creation," Gram said. "Built by the *Teth* early on as a sort of layover for travelers. It started as one small cabin, eons ago, and grew over time to become a safe haven, for those who could find it. Not just *Teth*, either. Though that is mostly who you will find here."

As I looked, I could see hundreds of people through windows or on their balconies. I felt a weird mixture of dread and excitement as I looked at them. I was going to meet more *Teth!* Other than Gram, I'd never met any *Teth* at all. And now I might meet *hundreds*. It made me feel a little sick to my stomach, nervous about how they'd see me or treat me.

"They're going to be very interested in you," Gram said, turning to look me in the eye. "You stay close. All *Teth* are welcome here, but not all have good intentions."

I nodded. "Standard Disney World protocol," I said.

Gramps burst out laughing, loud and sharp, and Gram frowned at him and then at me. "I'm never going to live that down, am I?"

"You acted like that trip was some kind of military operation," Gramps laughed.

"It was my first time. Also, I wasn't very impressed. It wasn't very grand, for a 'world.'"

"Well, it *is* a small world, after all," Gramps said, grinning.

I smiled, too. I was still nervous, but I'd handle it, somehow. Having Gram and Gramps with me would make things easier. What was the difference, really, between being here or being in a foreign country back on Earth Prime? Different customs. Different culture. But as long as I was with my family, I'd be ok. I repeated this to myself over and over.

We took the main road to the cabin, and entered through a large door in the front. Inside, it resembled a sort of hotel lobby. It was well lit, with electric lights. I hadn't expected that. I was imagining flickering torches or oily lamps. All the high fantasy I'd read had lied to me. "It's more modern than I expected," I said.

Gram laughed. "Define 'modern.' This place hasn't changed much in a thousand years."

A couple of people walked by, chatting with each other. They were holding what looked like smart phones or little handheld computers, tapping away at the screens, discussing what they were seeing there. Another man was sitting at a table in one corner, near what looked like a buffet. He had a laptop, and was typing away, unaware of anything else around him. Others in the room had devices I didn't recognize, and were doing things I couldn't quite wrap my head around. Maybe most disjointed of all, some really *did* look like something out of a fantasy book. They were dressed in animal skins or hand-woven textiles, and were playing dice or eating from big bowls using their hands as utensils. Oddly, seeing this made me feel better.

I shook my head. "Ok. So, what now?"

"Now we get a room, and we put the word out. Xander is probably here already."

Gram went to the front desk, or the bar, or whatever it was, as Gramps and I took a seat at one of the tables in the common area.

Unlike the hotels I was used to, this place had a sort of eclectic informality to it. The room was more or less wide open, though the space was occasionally broken by ornate wooden support columns. There was a large wooden staircase that looked like a large, spiraling oak tree growing through the ceiling. Here and there were walls that sectioned off some of the space, mostly providing small but private rooms for tables, where I imagined dark conversations about unspeakable things might happen regularly.

I watched as Gram approached the front desk, and the innkeeper seemed to know her. They chatted for a few minutes before I saw him give a shrug and shake his head a little. She came back with a sour look on her face.

"He hasn't seen Xander," she said. "And he wants us to leave our weapons at the front desk."

"Why?" Gramps asked.

"New policy. There was a dust-up here a while back. A *Teth* wizard was run through, and even though everyone seemed to appreciate it, the management cracked down. This is supposed to be a safe haven. So, no weapons."

Gramps shrugged and handed over his spear. I did the same. Gram took them up front, and handed them over. The guy behind the desk pointed at her hip, where she was wearing the hidden scabbard and sword. Apparently her camouflage wasn't enough to keep him from spotting it. The debate got a little heated, and Gramps groaned. "I knew she'd pull this. Wait here," and he went to help calm things down before someone ended up stabbed.

I settled in, leaning with my elbows on the table in front of me. It had been a long night, and we hadn't really slept. Plus we had marched along on that very long walk through the woods to get here. I was thinking about how much I could use a nap.

"They frown on people drowsing at the tables," a man said from the next table over.

I straightened, shaking my head a bit to perk up. "Thanks," I said, trying not to engage too much. *Standard Disney World protocol.*

"You look like you were dragged here behind a Pallump," he said.

I wanted to ignore him. I did. But curiosity was always my downfall. "What's a Pallump?" I asked.

"Oh, a great big mess of a beast!" the man said, gesturing and pantomiming a huge figure with his hands. "Three legs, all of them thicker than a tree trunk and covered in thick hair. Hairy trees!" he laughed. "They move pretty fast for a tri-ped, but they're a bit off balance. Running and walking are more or less a process of controlled crash landing for a Pallump. They make a heck of a mess as they go."

"That sounds about right," I said, nodding and smiling, trying to back out of the conversation gracefully.

"Nothing right about a Pallump," the man said, ignoring my subtle cues. "They eat too much, and tend to vomit everywhere. They groom a lot when they aren't running, so they produce these huge, gooey hairballs. And they produce absolute mountains of poo."

I stifled a laugh. "I'll avoid them. Thanks for the warning."

"Avoid! You should *see* one! I think there's one in the stables out back, want to have a peek?"

I hesitated, then shook my head. "That sounds a little creepy," I said.

He thought for a second. "*Should* probably sound creepy, when someone asks you to take a peek at a Pallump in the stables out back.

It's legit, though. So, you came here from pretty far away. I'm guessing one of the more boring Layers. Something with TV, I bet. Am I right?"

"How'd you know that?" I asked.

"You registered no shock at all. I tell *you* about a three-legged beast covered in hair and you're more amused by the mountain of poo it makes. Could only be TV. Desensitizes you to nonsense."

I smiled. I couldn't help myself. "You've been to a lot of Layers with TV?" I asked.

"As many as I can visit at a time, absolutely! I'm addicted to 'Gilligan's Island.' Ever seen it?"

"It's pretty old. I've seen reruns."

He leaned in, his intensity amping up, and whispered, "Did they ever make it off that island?" Suddenly he leaned back, throwing his hands up as if guarding himself. "Don't tell me! No spoilers!"

I laughed, though I didn't want to. I wanted to turn away, to keep observing the Disney World protocol — stick to the group, avoid engaging with strangers, eat my ice cream slowly. Ice cream sounded really good right now.

But I couldn't help myself. I hadn't had many opportunities to "make friends" in my life. At sixteen (going on seventeen … I was always "going on" one age or another), I hadn't had a lot of chances to even meet new people. Gram and Gramps didn't keep me shuttered in the house, and we did make trips from time to time. But it was mostly the three of us. My friendships tended to be short-lived.

Suddenly I saw something move under the flap of the man's bag, which was sitting in the chair next to him. It looked like a worn leather messenger bag.

"Got a puppy in there?" I asked, nodding to his bag. "Maybe a Pallump puppy?"

He looked at the bag and scowled. "No. And Pallumps have kids, not puppies. That's not a kid or a puppy, though." He leaned toward his bag and, speaking to it more than to me, said, "It's a ridiculous annoyance that doesn't follow orders, 'Lay there and don't move. Half an hour, that's all I ask.' Might as well have asked it for the secret to Michael Bay's success, for all that's worth."

"You know Michael Bay?" I asked.

"Scourge of the Omniverse? Destroyer of childhood dreams? Oh yes. *Everyone* knows and despises Michael Bay."

I nodded. "Transformers."

"Exactly!"

I nodded to the bag again. "So despite every rule I'm supposed to follow and every book I've ever read or movie I've ever seen … what's in the bag?"

He smiled. "You're not a rule follower?"

I shrugged. "I can neither confirm nor deny."

He chuckled. "Ok. Well, my little friend isn't much of a rule follower either. But for now, I think he'd better stay hidden. Too many people recognize him. Besides, I think your Gram and Gramps are coming back."

I blinked. "How did you …"

"I've known them, and you, for a very long time," He smiled. "Sawyer Jackson."

I felt a shock go through me, only for a second, and was about to say something when I heard Gram say, "Xander!"

What followed was bizarre.

Gram squealed like a little girl, and ran to Xander, who rose from his chair. In a most un-Gram way, she leapt up and wrapped herself around him, like a young girl hugging her boyfriend.

I glanced at Gramps, who did not look nearly as thrilled. He had a sour expression on his face, as if he'd tasted something disgusting.

He really is jealous, I thought. All the play and banter between him and

Gram, all the comments about Xander, and I had assumed he was mostly kidding. Gram did too, I think. But there it was, plain and open, right on his face. I didn't even need to read the knotwork to see it.

When Gram disentangled herself and smoothed her clothes and hair, she entwined her arm in Xander's and turned to face me, smiling. *Beaming.* "I see you two have already met."

"Oh, I tried to corrupt him, but it seems he's already corrupted," Xander said.

"He gets that from his Gram," Gramps said, stepping forward and holding out a stiff hand to Xander.

Xander shook his head, "We've been through too much for that, Drew," he said, and pulled Gramps into a hearty hug that might have snapped a few ribs. To my surprise, Gramps chuckled and hugged back, patting Xander's back in solid claps. The hug actually did seem kind of warm, making me wonder at the complexity of the whole relationship. What would it be like to both like someone and not like them at the same time?

They pulled away, and Xander reached out and snagged his bag, pulling it over one shoulder. He was dressed in fairly normal clothes for an immortal Exemplar, I thought. Though I didn't know what an Exemplar should look like, exactly. He was supposed to be the "ultimate human," though, and in that he wasn't quite what I was expecting. He was maybe six foot, give or take an inch, with short, dark hair that was spiked in a casual sort of style, and occasionally picked up highlights from the electric bulbs in the wall fixtures.

Xander's eyes were sort of a mystery. I couldn't quite get an idea of the color. They were a sort of grey when we met, almost a light blue, but now seemed more green. Hazel, maybe.

He was thin, but not skinny. Muscular, I was guessing, but not a bodybuilder. More like someone who ran a lot. Probably out of necessity. And his clothes were functional while still managing to be stylish looking. He wore a short brown coat, maybe a light wool or camel hair, that hit around mid-thigh. It had large, copper-looking buttons on the front. As he and my grandparents chatted, I saw a glimpse of the lining, which made me do a double take.

Just from my brief look, it seemed his coat was lined with hundreds of buttons, in every color and size you could imagine.

"My little friend almost gave me away," Xander said, nodding to the bag. "He's getting impatient. Can we go up to the rooms?"

"We're on seven," Gram said.

"Ah, seven! You spared no expense!"

"The rooms are free, Xander," Gram said, smiling.

"Of course they are. But you picked the best."

"Wouldn't the top floor be the best?" Gramps said. "Everyone always wants the top floor."

"You've never been snapped up by a giant robot bird that rips through the ceiling and grabs you in its metal beak," Xander said.

"Well, no. I think most people may have that flaw," Gramps said, rolling his eyes

"To seven!" Xander led the way, bag slung over his shoulder.

Gram followed immediately, and Gramps and I exchanged looks as we stepped in behind. Xander led us to a wall lined with doors, and as one set opened we stepped into what turned out to be an elevator.

Or, it was *functionally* an elevator. It looked more like an ornate wooden cage, finely carved from a single piece of wood. There was a twisting sort of motif woven throughout the design. I looked at it in the knotwork, and the story it told was one of safety and stability. I could see a thick line of cable above us, visible as glowing knotwork, that lifted the elevator and moved it along. The line branched off in different directions, not just straight up and down, and in a moment we veered onto one of these sidelines, gliding sideways until the elevator stopped and the door slid open.

"That was different than normal," I said.

"Normal depends on your point of view," Xander said. "Your point of view is going to change a lot soon. And often."

I shot a glance at Gram and Gramps. Gram was smiling and looking at Xander. Gramps was scowling, and looking at Xander. No help there.

We entered a large room that contained a couple of beds, a table with four chairs, and a large armoire. There was a sofa on one end, and a small bar in the corner. No kitchenette or sink, which I was starting to expect. The place really was a sort of hotel.

Gramps went straight to the bar.

"Drew, really?" Gram asked.

"If we're going to do this, I need my wits anywhere but about me," Gramps said. He rustled behind the bar and came up with a large, clear bottle filled with brown liquid. He pulled a stopper out of it, found a glass behind the bar, and poured a couple of fingers. He held this up to Xander, raising an eyebrow.

Xander, a gleam in his eye, nodded. Gramps handed him the glass, and poured another for himself. Gram rolled her eyes.

I was secretly hoping they'd offer me something. No such luck.

"So," Xander said, after taking a sip and making a slight face. "Not Scotch," he said.

Gramps took a sip, and smacked his lips a bit. "Rum?"

"Similar," Xander said. "Maybe something from one of the all-tropical Layers."

"Has a bit of spice to it," Gramps said.

"Would you two please wrap this up?" Gram asked, exasperated. "You don't know what the foul liquid is, you're going to drink it anyway. Carry on."

"So," Xander said again. "Seems our boy brought back a snare and alerted half the Omni to where he was hiding."

"I didn't mean to," I said. "But, yeah, that's pretty much it."

Xander smiled. "It happens. Or, well, it doesn't just *happen*. Snares don't latch on to just anybody. You … they're *hunting* for you."

"On account of me being 'the Chosen,' I guess."

Xander laughed. "Someone's been watching a lot of movies."

"All the movies," I said. "And all the books. I'm a walking 'Hero's Journey.' Joseph Campbell would be proud. So what do we do?"

Xander arched an eyebrow and looked at Gram. "He's very *take charge*, isn't he?"

Gram had a strange sort of tight-lipped smile on her face. "I guess he is at that."

"You raised him, Liv," Gramps said, raising his glass in toast.

"We both did,'" she said, and moved closer to the bar, leaning over and kissing him on the lips. I cringed.

Xander motioned for me to have a seat at the table, which I did. He sat across from me. Gram and Gramps stayed at the bar. I waited for whatever was about to happen next, feeling a little anxiety about how *unsure* I was. So much had happened, and so quickly, I wasn't certain I could trust how I was feeling about it. There was a sort of numbness taking hold of me. Not so numb that I couldn't think. More like a resolve — that whatever weird was happening, it was happening whether I wanted it to or not. So why not flow with it?

"You're not afraid at *all*, are you?" Xander said. I could hear a bit of marvel in his voice, though I wasn't sure why.

"I'm afraid," I said. "Very afraid. But that doesn't do me any good. I have to make sure I stay clear."

"Clear," Xander said, nodding. "No freak outs. That's what your Gram taught you."

I nodded.

He looked at me for a moment, then reached into his bag, which he had placed on the floor next to him. He pulled out a small, black sphere and brought it up to the table. He held it in the air, just above the table's surface, and then let it go. Instead of dropping to the table, however, it just floated there, where he'd released it, and slowly it turned in mid-air.

It was a magic 8-ball.

"This is 8-Ball," Xander said.

"I … ok. I gathered that," I said.

He smirked. "Well, that's the name it goes by right now. It picked this form a long time ago, before I even knew what an 8-ball was. It did it just to annoy me, I'm convinced."

"And what does it do?" I asked.

"It *knows* everything," Xander replied. "But good luck getting it to share anything useful. It only answers the way an 8-ball would answer. Cryptic little annoying answers that tell me nothing."

I nodded. "Signs point to yes," I said.

"Yes! You've heard of it then. Good. Because 8-Ball only answers that way, even though it knows everything that ever can be known. It's actually the Akashic record in a physical form. The Akashic Sphere."

"The what?"

Gramps answered from behind the bar, "The Akashic record is sort of a legendary record of all knowledge," he said. "The word 'akashic' means 'sky' or 'ether.' There's a lot of spiritual mumbo-jumbo around it, but it really boils down to physics. There's this notion in quantum mechanics …"

Gram interrupted him. "There's an all-knowing sphere hovering above that table and you *still* think you're the smartest living thing in the room!" Gram said, punching him in the arm.

Gramps rubbed his arm, where a bruise would surely form later. "Point taken," he said.

"As I was saying," Xander continued, "8-Ball knows everything. But he's finicky about sharing information or answering questions.

He may only give you one shot, or ten. And his answers are going to frustrate you to the point of wanting to use a blowtorch on him."

I looked at Xander, then to Gram and Gramps, and back again. "What am I supposed to ask him?" I asked.

Xander shrugged. "That's up to you."

"I don't have any questions."

Xander's eyebrows shot up. "You've just learned that the universe isn't the only universe, that there's an Omniverse of realities out there that contain wonders you could never have imagined, that you were more or less created by the knotwork after the *Teth* found out about some big, bad event that you're meant to prevent or put a stop to — but you have *no questions?*"

I thought about this. Actually, the truth was I had *too many* questions. I just didn't know where to start. Nothing I really *wanted* to ask would get very good results. *Why me?* seemed like a waste of time. *What next?* wasn't any better. But those were the questions pressing against the inside of my brain, straining to get out, but they just didn't seem *worthy*.

Then a question occurred to me.

I turned to face 8-Ball, and asked, "What is the big event I was born to prevent?"

8-Ball hovered, then started to shake in mid-air, as if someone had it in their hands and was giving it a go. After a couple of seconds, it rotated, showing me the little window where the answer to my question would appear.

"Concentrate and ask again," I read out loud. I looked up at Xander.

"He does that," Xander said, shrugging. "Ask again. Try to concentrate on what you really need to know."

I thought about it, and then tried a different approach. "Will the event happen soon?"

Again, 8-Ball shook in mid-air, and turned to reveal the answer.

"As I see it, yes," I read. I followed up quickly, "Will I succeed?"

8-Ball shook, and answered.

"Don't count on it," I read. For the first time, I felt a chill go through me.

"That may not mean what you think it means," Xander said. "Remember, 8-Ball knows everything. It's answering your questions in a very limited way, because it also knows that too much information about the future can be bad. It's best to keep your questions centered on here and now, instead of trying to glean information about the future. Things change too rapidly for the future to be really *known*, anyway. But 8-Ball may also be telling you that success isn't necessarily your goal."

"Why wouldn't success be my goal?" I asked.

Xander shrugged. "Who knows? That's why 8-Ball drives me nuts. He's followed me for more years than most Layers have existed, and I feel like he's as much a mystery as the first day I met him."

I had a whole lot of questions then, but all of them would have to be answered by Xander, not 8-Ball. Gram and Gramps could do with answering a few questions, too. But before I got into all of that, I had one more question for the Akashic Sphere.

"Will I ever have a normal life again?"

8-Ball shook, and out of the corner of my eye I saw Gram and Gramps trade glances. When 8-Ball finally turned to show me the little screen, I almost didn't want to read it.

"Better not tell you now," I read. I threw my hands up. "What the heck does *that* mean?" I said, a little louder than I had intended.

"Told ya," Xander smirked.

I pushed away from the table, a little disgusted. "What was the point of that?" I asked.

"I wanted to see what you'd ask him," Xander said. "And what he'd say in response."

"Why?" I asked.

"It's important to know where your head is. No better way to know that than to listen to the questions you think matter most."

I looked at him for a moment, then sank down and sat on the end of one of the beds before laying back. The bed was soft and inviting. I felt a sort of warmth come over me. A quick glance at the knotwork of the bed revealed that it told a story of rest and peaceful sleep. All I wanted was to agree to that story, to let it be *my* story for a while.

I was starting to doze when I heard Gram say, "He's been through a lot, Xander. Is he ready for this?"

"He has to be," Xander said. "8-Ball isn't being coy. I think the event is happening soon. I think it's no accident that Sawyer found a way to travel to the Long Land, all on his own. He's one of the most powerful *Teth* I've ever seen. And he's smart. He takes all of this better than even I would, I think."

"He's always been pretty level headed," Gramps said.

"It's more than that," Xander said. "He's got a stronger bond to the knotwork than any *Teth* I've ever met. I may not be able to see the knotwork directly, but I've been around long enough to see how it effects people. He's tied to it tighter than anyone I've ever known. Maybe more than Aeodymus himself."

I recognized the name immediately, even in my sleepy haze. *Am I like Aeodymus?* I thought. I didn't know much about him, other than the fact that he had set himself up as some sort of god, and he used his ability with the knotwork to do evil things, tearing holes in the fabric of reality the whole time. I knew that he sent the Inks after us, to try to kill us, or kidnap us — I wasn't sure which at that moment. If I was like Aeodymus, in the abilities I possessed, would I eventually become like him in other ways? Would I abuse my power? Become evil?

I wouldn't let that happen. No matter what this "event" turned out to be, I was going to stop it. I would do whatever it took to make sure everyone stayed safe, even if it meant I died trying.

"What about tomorrow?" Gram asked. "We can't stay here long. There are too many spies around. There are bound to be wizards."

"I wish you'd stop calling them that," Gramps complained. "It makes them sound like something out of Harry Potter. What they do is science, not magic."

"It's the word we use," Gram shrugged. "You know that. Just be thankful we're not dealing with any gods."

"Also not a word I like," Gramps said.

"No one likes the gods," Xander said. "But I haven't encountered any recently. They're scurrying all over the Layers, causing all kinds of rips and tears, but they're keeping ahead of me so far."

"So again," Gram said. "What about tomorrow? We have to keep moving, but I don't know if we can stay in the Long Land."

"You can, actually," Xander said. "But *he* can't."

There was a pause. "What do you mean?" Gram asked, her voice quiet.

"I need to take Sawyer with me tomorrow morning. There's a task he'll need to accomplish. 8-Ball was vague, as always, but led me to a couple of things that Sawyer needs to do. You'll stay behind, here in the Long Land, and try to throw everyone off of the trail. Move around all you like, but you'll need to come back to the Cabin every now and then. I'll send word when we're on our way back."

"What about snares?" Gramps asked. I could hear tension in his voice. "Every time he moves through the Layers, doesn't he trigger some kind of ripple or something?"

Xander replied, "I can move using the buttons. You *Teth* can't track that. It's outside of the knotwork."

"You are *not* taking my boy gallivanting all over the Layers!" Gramps said.

"It's for the best, Drew," Xander said. "And I think we both know

I will take him, because I have to. If you want him to be safe, he goes with me."

I heard a sniffling sound, and for a second I tried to stir, to open my eyes and sit up. But it was too late. This conversation was registering just as I was fading, drifting into sleep. I was already out, for all intents and purposes. It seemed suspicious — and I wondered, in those fading moments, if Gram had done something to the knotwork to make me sleep.

"I can't bear to let him go," Gram said.

There was the shuffling sound of someone moving, and Gramps said, "It's ok, Liv. He'll be ok. Xander will protect him." He paused, and when he spoke again his voice was harder than I'd ever heard it. "Because if he doesn't, there is nowhere in the Omni where he'll be safe."

"Fair enough," Xander said.

If the conversation continued after that, I didn't hear a word of it.

SIX | BUTTONS

Gram was crying, and she wouldn't let the hug end.

"I'll be fine, Gram," I said. Though I wasn't at all sure that I would be fine. I wasn't sure of anything. I'd spent my entire life with Gram and Gramps — I couldn't remember another life, nor any other parents. They were it. They were my world.

But Xander was right.

I wasn't sure why I knew, but I knew. Xander's plan wasn't just the best plan for keeping me alive, it was the best plan for keeping Gram and Gramps safe as well. They might be in some danger, if anyone was following them. But they were in even more danger if I was with them. I had to go, and they had to stay.

Besides, 8-Ball had said there were some things I needed to accomplish, to make myself ready for whatever was coming. That sounded exciting and fun, but it also sounded like something I really needed.

"We'd better get moving," Xander said. "While it's still dark." He was dressed in the same clothes he'd worn the day before, with the strap of his bag over one shoulder. 8-Ball hovered near him. It had refused to go back into the bag, no matter how sternly Xander asked.

I pulled away from Gram and stood next to Xander. 8-Ball came floating my way, hovering just off of my left shoulder. I wasn't entirely sure about the Akashic Sphere. It was strange and quiet. It knew everything, but told you practically nothing. Except, as it hovered there, next to me, it felt like it was talking to me the whole time, telling me it liked me, that I was doing the right thing.

I looked at it in the knotwork, and almost jerked my head away. There were so many threads weaving in and out of 8-Ball, so many lines spiraling off into space, it was like staring into a sun. Nothing I'd seen so far was so well connected to *everything*. And the story coming from its knotwork was endless and rambling. All knowledge — everything known or ever to be known, in every universe in the Omni — 8-Ball's story was the story of everything.

I was dressed in new clothes, something more fitting for travel. I still wore my jeans, but in place of my sneakers was a pair of old boots that Xander had given me from his bag. They were oddly comfortable, form-fitting to my feet, providing ankle support without being too tight. And they looked cool, which may have been the only thing that really mattered.

Xander had also given me a bag, similar to his, with a single leather strap that I had slung over my neck and shoulder, hanging the bag at my side. I looked into it, to see what kind of provisions I had.

I blinked.

The bag was filled with all kinds of things. More than I could have imagined. Just at a glance I could see a rolled up sleeping bag, a pillow, a couple of pairs of jeans, some shirts, a canteen, a few containers of food, some rope, a flashlight, my sneakers and T-shirt, some books — the more I looked, the more I saw. Yet the bag felt light as a feather. Not only that …

"It's huge in there," I said. "It's … it's bigger on the inside!"

Xander nodded. "A little trick I picked up from a Doctor I met once. There's a small pocket universe in there. Or rather, you're carrying a bag that contains nothing but the mouth of a gateway that leads to a small pocket universe. Took me centuries to figure out how to build it."

Gramps was peeking over my shoulder to get a look into the bag. "Mind sharing how you did it?" he asked.

"Maybe some other time," Xander said.

"In other words, 'no,'" Gramps grumbled.

Xander smiled.

Gram rushed up and hugged me one more time. "You be careful. Don't get into any trouble. And if you do get into trouble, just hold your necklace and whisper my name. The knotwork will carry that to me."

I nodded. "Ok. Cool."

She smiled. "And the braid will tell you stories of our bloodline, if you ask. So ask. It's not quite the same as us being there, but maybe you'll learn something useful."

"Ok," I said again. Maybe that would keep me from feeling homesick, but I doubted it. The whole experience was too strange and too new. Just having access to information wasn't going to keep me from feeling isolated.

Gramps stepped up then and pulled me into a quick hug. "You've got your pocket knife?" he asked.

"Yessir," I said, digging it out of the watch pocket of my jeans.

"Keep it handy. All this knotwork stuff is fine, but nothing beats a Swiss Army knife when you're in a spot."

I nodded and put it back in my pocket, then turned to Xander. "Are we going back through the forest?" I asked.

He looked confused. "Why would we do that?" he asked.

I shrugged. "So how are we leaving? I haven't really opened a gate on purpose yet. I can try …"

"I've got it covered," he said, reaching inside his coat. He grabbed one of the buttons sewn there, gave it a quick tug, and snapped the threads, pulling it free. He looked at Gram and Gramps. "After we're gone, pack up and leave suddenly. I think there are at least a couple of wizards staying here. I didn't set off any snares, but they may not have realized who I was. They'll be looking for all three of you by now, so give them someone to chase. Leave while it's dark."

Gram nodded. "We'll swing by and pick up the weapons. They're probably monitoring the front desk."

Xander turned to me. "Ready?" he asked.

I nodded, and then watched as he reached out in front of him, with the button in his hand. What he did next was strange, even in light of everything else that had happened. The best way to describe it is to say that he "unbuttoned" the space in front of us, creating an opening like a piece of cloth falling away to reveal an opening.

I stared, and then bent to look at the piece of "fabric" dangling loose to one side of the opening. I could see, within its folds, the scene that should have been there in place of the hole in mid-air. It was as if the light from that spot had bent and folded, as if I were looking at a print of that space instead of the space itself.

"Come along, Sawyer," Xander said, and stepped through the hole.

8-Ball bumped my shoulder, nudging me, and I snapped out of it and started to follow Xander through. I turned to look at Gram and Gramps one last time. "I'll miss you," I said, feeling my throat get tight and my eyes burn.

"Miss you too, kid," Gramps said.

"Be careful!" Gram yelled.

In an instant, I was through the hole, and standing next to Xander on a strange new Layer. He turned then, and rebuttoned the "fabric." He held the button out to me, in the palm of his hand, and I watched as it blackened and turned to dust before sifting away.

"I have no idea what I just saw," I said.

"And yet it doesn't seem to faze you much. I was hoping for at least a 'cool' or 'tubular' or something."

"'Tubular?' Has anyone ever actually said that?"

"Doesn't everyone? It's fly, right?"

I shook my head, and smiled in spite of myself. And I was grateful. Because if not for this nonsense, I might have cried, and crying definitely did not feel right in this place.

"Where are we?" I asked, looking around.

We were standing on a paved walkway that ran along the side of a large, glass building. High above, dipping and diving and whizzing by at ridiculous speeds, I saw hundreds of flying vehicles. Looking closer, they seemed like cars more than airplanes or helicopters. They were *everywhere*.

"I don't really know the name of the place, but isn't it cool?"

"Don't you mean tubular?" I asked.

"Nothing is tubular. Get hip. But *this* place! It's cool! Flying *cars*! Do you know how rare that is? It's possible on almost every technologically advanced world, and yet the local governments do everything they can to block it from happening. Same thing with organic energy, instead of non-replenishing fuels. One of the things I love about this Layer."

"Are we hiding out here?" I asked. The prospect of exploring a world with flying cars was kind of exciting. I wondered what other technology they might have. Gramps would have loved this place.

"Not for long. We're here to pick up something I left here."

"What?" I asked.

Instead of answering, Xander strode away, practically leaning forward as he walked. I tripped a little as I took a step after him, but corrected and followed as closely as I could. "Where are we going?" I asked.

"To the heart of the Layer," he said. "It's not far. I buttoned us in pretty close. Would have gone straight there, but I'm never sure if anyone's watching, and I want to avoid attention."

I said nothing to that. What *could* I say? I only really understood half of it anyway.

Instead I followed Xander until we came to a another large building of gleaming glass, towering high into the sky. Hundreds of flying cars were clustered around it at the very top.

"Are we going up there?" I asked, quietly. I was somewhat awed by its height.

Xander stopped and looked up, admiring. "Beautiful, isn't it? But no." He continued marching on, straight for a set of doors in the base of the building. He got to these and started patting the pockets of his coat. Eventually he pulled out a small plastic card, waved it in front of a panel by the doors, and then reached out and grabbed the handle, giving it a yank.

Nothing happened.

Xander hesitated, swiped the card again, then yanked.

Nothing.

He looked at the card closely. "This thing can't expire," he said. "It's the ultimate access card. It comes from the Long Land! It's like the access card all other access cards are based on!"

I looked at the door, and the panel, and then the card. On a whim I looked at all three in the knotwork, and saw immediately that the card had a different pattern than the lock. "It's the wrong card," I said.

"Wrong card?" Xander asked, incredulous. "Oh! Yeah, ok. Hold on," and again he patted his pockets until he produced another card, identical to the first. "Sorry. Different reality."

He swiped the new card, and this time I heard a loud *click* from the doors. Xander pulled the handle and the door came open instantly.

"Thanks!" Xander said, just before striding into the building. I followed quickly, with 8-Ball right behind me, and squeezed through before the door could shut. I tripped a little on the threshold, and 8-Ball zipped over my head and into the room as I straightened and stood to look around. I gaped in awe as the door automatically closed behind me.

Inside was … different than I had expected.

It was immense, for starters, and had an industrial feel, with pipes and wires running in neat and orderly rows along the ceiling, in and out of ports and conduits in the walls. Large machines spanned the room as far as I could see — these must have been the machinery that kept the entire building running. I could see panels and machines that were clearly for electrical, climate control, lighting, plumbing controls and more.

Despite mechanics and technology of the place, however, there was something *organic* about all of it. I looked at the knotwork, and saw that streams of glowing life flowed and twisted, making a strange pattern that spoke of utility and practical purpose. This was a *living* machine.

"What do you think?" Xander asked. He was standing by a door that led to a small room across from where we had entered. He had the door open, and was paused in the act of stepping through, watching me watch the room.

I looked around again, then back to Xander. "It's alive," I said, a bit of awe in my voice. "How is it alive?"

Xander smiled. "Living machines. This universe figured out the balance early. One of the reasons I love this place so much. It was one of the first Layers I had to restitch, back a few thousand years ago. One of the *Teth* wizards had shredded it, playing god and making a bunch of commands." He affected a faux deep voice and said, "'Behold my power to turn people into metal automatons!' That sort of thing. He used the knotwork to create a bunch of robot slaves, who served as his army. Paid no attention to their stories, tore holes into the fabric all over the place. All kinds of things leaked in from the outside, which only served to cement his hold on the people. They thought he was all-powerful, bringing demons from the beyond. Schmuck."

"But you fixed all those tears?" I asked.

"It wasn't easy," he said. "But yes. It took centuries to patch all the holes and restitch this place. But I wasn't able to change back the automatons, unfortunately. I don't have the ability to work with the knotwork, the way you do. And at the time, I didn't trust any *Teth*. They all seemed corrupt with power. It wasn't until years later I met people from your bloodline, who seemed pretty decent."

"So those robot people had to live out their lives that way? Stuck as robots?"

Xander regarded me for a moment, then gave a light nod. "Yes. Some of them are actually still around, believe it or not. They're honored here. Living machines. It was because of that idiot's play for godhood that these people discovered that technology and life do not have to be separate. They learned from his atrocities, and turned it into something good."

I thought about this. I liked it, as a notion. Learning to build something good from a nightmare. That seemed like a good way to live, to me. I'd have to remember it.

"So now what?" I asked. "What are we looking for here?"

Xander didn't answer, but instead nodded his head toward the door and went through with me and 8-Ball trailing behind.

The room wasn't a room at all, but a stairwell that apparently ran behind a bank of elevators. The stairs spiraled up and down from here. Below, as I peered over a rail, the stairwell ran deeper and deeper. Xander was already a flight below me. "Is this building bigger on the inside, like my bag?" I called down.

Without pausing, Xander called back up, "No, just really, really big! Now come along, Sawyer. There's something I want to show you!"

I glanced upward one more time, then followed. 8-Ball hovered along with me as I went, which felt oddly comforting.

Gravity helped quite a bit in keeping me going, flight after flight. Even with that momentum, however, I was getting worn out by the constant step-by-step movement. Several floors down I stopped, huffing. "Xander!" I called down the shaft.

I saw him peek up at me, about three floors down. "I'm beat," I said. "Can we take a break?"

He smiled. "We're almost there, I promise! Catch up. Use the knotwork!" And with that I heard the sound of his footsteps pounding downward once again.

Use the knotwork. What did that mean? So far, I'd managed to figure a few things out about the knotwork, mostly by accident. I was able to manipulate it, to tie my own pattern into other objects and create something new. I wasn't sure how to do anything useful just yet, though. I had so far managed to accidentally travel to the Long Land, where I'd picked up a snare without even realizing it. I had also completely destroyed an Ink by cutting its knotwork pattern to shreds. I'd made a couple of spears look invisible. Beyond that, What else could I do?

I'd gotten pretty good at "knotwork vision." I could turn it on and off at will. Having it "on" full-time had been a little disorienting. But I found I was switching modes frequently, checking things out as I went, like pulling down a pair of sunglasses to see the world unfiltered. What I hadn't done yet was experiment, to see if I could do things the way Gram could. She had the ability to create a whole new knotwork, with its own story entwined in it. I wasn't sure how to do that, exactly, other than small-scale things like camouflage. And worse, I wasn't sure how to do it without crossing the line and becoming like the "wizards" or "gods" that Xander and my grandparents had told me about. What if I tore a hole in reality?

They hadn't told me much about *how* these *Teth* managed to tear holes in reality, but based on the stories I'd heard so far I had a notion. I was guessing it had something to do with forcing the knotwork into a pattern that worked against something's *natural* pattern. Or, maybe, forcing it into a pattern it just didn't *want* to be in. Being able to see the knotwork, I knew one thing for certain about it — the whole thing was alive. The Omniverse, with its clusters of multiverses, was a living thing. The knotwork was the life of it.

If it was alive, and a *Teth* used his abilities to force it into a shape it didn't want to be in, then it would resist, and that could be what caused the tears in reality that Xander had to patch up.

But what if it didn't mind the story I was trying to tell? What if it didn't mind the pattern I had in mind? How could I know?

I could ask.

Why not? The knotwork pattern — wasn't that a form of communication? Ever since discovering the knotwork, I'd been "reading" stories from it, like little whispers of what the pattern meant. And the few times I had manipulated the knotwork myself, I was more or less forming shapes that made sense to me, telling the story I wanted to tell, using the knotwork to give that story power.

I looked at my own knotwork, which was not exactly easy to do. It's a little like trying to stare at the end of your own nose. You can see some of it, but not all. Unfortunately there were no mirrors I could use, so the best I could do was to look down and gather in as much of my pattern as I could.

Unlike the other times I had examined the knotwork, this time I was looking for a specific story. I wanted to see that part of me that was tired and wanted to rest. This wasn't quite as simple as just letting the knotwork "speak" to me. It was more like flipping through a book while looking for a specific passage.

It took a bit, but I finally spotted it — a dynamic bit of knotwork that spoke of being weary and needing to rest. I could see, though, that it wasn't quite "true." The message seemed to be more akin to "weary, but could keep going," and "need rest, but could keep moving." I took this to mean that I was tired, but it was more of a mental game.

I "reached out" then, to try to adjust my knotwork.

This was different than what I'd done before. I wasn't using my hands, for starters. Instead, I was concentrating on the knotwork, and sending a sort of mental image of what I was looking for. I was telling the knotwork a story, about being refreshed and invigorated and strong. I was telling the knotwork about being rested.

Slowly, very slowly, the knotwork began to change. It picked up the thread of my story, and shifted to match it, piece by piece. And as it did so, I could *feel it.*

At first it started as a sort of tingle, like excitement bubbling in my stomach. Gradually I felt a sort of calm come over my entire body, like a wave of liquid energy filling every cell. My muscles relaxed and the stiffness faded. My head cleared, a fog of sorts rising from it. I felt a lot like I'd just woken up, after a really good night's sleep.

8-Ball swung around and hovered in front of me. It shook, and when it revealed its "answer" I read, "Outlook good."

I smiled. "Thanks, 8-Ball. You're lookin' good yourself."

Feeling much better, and with a lot more pep in my step, I started down the stairs again. I wanted to catch up to Xander, so I started sprinting, taking two steps at a time, with 8-Ball keeping pace by my side.

To my surprise, I was racing along and not feeling the slightest bit tired. In fact, the longer this went on, the better I seemed to feel. I was breathing heavily, of course. I could still feel the exertion. But it didn't bother me. I was feeling good.

I rounded one turn in the stairs and stopped short, seeing Xander leaning against the wall next to the door. "About time you showed up!" he said. "Feeling better, I see."

"Yeah," I said, smiling.

"Some of us have to tromp through the world the old fashioned way," he said.

"Very, very, *very* old fashioned, in your case," I said.

Xander arched his eyebrows. "Have we finally gotten to the banter stage? Good! I was worried you were going to be boring and whiny. Well, fine then. Let's get moving before I turn to dust or something."

He winked at me, and then opened the door and barreled through without waiting.

The room we entered was ridiculous.

Not in a bad way. It was more that it just seemed *unreal*. It was filled to every corner with plants and trees, for starters. Above, the ceiling was some sort of faux sky, with "sunlight" filtering through clouds and leaves. But it was the *sound* that made the whole thing surreal. I could hear crickets, birds, small animals in the brush, the sound of a stream or small waterfall somewhere. The room reminded me a little of the clearing in the woods behind my house, back on Earth Prime. The thought of it gave me a touch of homesickness.

"I know I say this a lot, but I was not expecting this," I said.

Xander laughed. "No, I suppose you wouldn't. He likes to surround himself with life and nature. He hasn't left this room in a very long time."

"He who?" I asked.

Xander didn't answer, but instead pointed ahead.

I looked, not sure at first what he was indicating, but then eventually made out a copper-colored figure standing in some of the taller grass. He was completely motionless, but I could see by his knotwork that he was very much alive.

That wasn't all I could see.

His knotwork was *wrong*. It began with one story, but was horribly twisted and mutilated into another. The knotwork, normally a bright line of light and life, was dark and purple, like a bruise or a scar. It looked painful, actually. And all around it were tatters, broken threads that dangled and hung loose, torn from the pattern they were meant to form and leading nowhere.

This was what gods and wizards could do. This was what it meant to tear the fabric of reality. Someone had forced this poor man into a shape he was never meant to be in. A shape he hadn't wanted.

"An automaton," I said, my voice just a whisper.

Xander nodded. "Yes. Edgar. He was transformed by the *Teth* who ruled this world as a god."

"How is he still alive?" I asked. "You said that was thousands of years ago."

Again Xander nodded. "Yes. When I repaired the Layer and got rid of that wizard, I had no way to return the automatons to normal. I've enlisted help from several *Teth*, since then, but none of it helped. Your own Gram tried. All of them told me the same thing. Retying Edgar's knotwork would likely kill him, but might also kill the *Teth* who tried. It's such a tangled mess, it looks to be impossible."

I studied Edgar and his knotwork. It was kind of sickening, to be honest. Seeing it, and hearing the mangled story of it, made me want to throw up, or cry, or scream in anger. It was sending so many messages of raw emotion, I didn't know what to listen to. I tried to block it out.

"Why are we here?" I asked, mostly to distract myself.

"Edgar has been kind enough to hold on to something for me. I'm here to retrieve it."

With that Xander walked toward Edgar, who remained motionless. If not for my ability to see and read the knotwork, and to know that he was fully aware of us, I might have thought he was just a statue.

I followed Xander, and as we stood in front of Edgar I watched as Xander reached out a hand.

Edgar reacted, then, reaching back rather slowly. His hand gripped Xander's, and the two of them shook in greeting. Xander released his hand and said, "It's good to see you, Edgar. I hope you're doing well."

I heard a light sort of grinding noise, like two rusted pieces of metal rubbing against each other. "I am well," Edgar said. His voice was measured, and maybe a little slow, but otherwise normal. The inflection was a little stiff, maybe. But on the whole, I was kind of surprised by how *human* he sounded.

"I'm glad to hear it!" Xander said, reaching out to chuck Edgar on the shoulder. "It's been too long. You've done wonders with the place," Xander looked around the room, taking it all in.

"You have come for the *Vivificantern*," Edgar said.

I looked at Xander, who glanced at me. "He's never been one for small talk," Xander said.

"Vivificantern?" I asked.

"Vivificantern is Latin for 'Life Giver.' I just call it 'Cantern' for short."

"What is it?" I asked.

Xander smiled, then turned back to Edgar. "Yes, that's what we're here for. Mind taking us to it?"

Edgar turned and walked deeper into the woods, with us following.

It was several minutes later before we stopped in front of a large tree. As I looked closer, however, I saw that it wasn't really a tree at all, but a large, thick column that *looked* like a tree. Where its branches would have reached into the sky, however, they terminated at the ceiling, and from there the image of the tree's top was presented as waving in a virtual breeze.

"Support column," Xander said. "Sort of a load-bearing beam. It's actually hollow."

"Ok," I said. There were just too many things for me to consider and pay attention to right now. The mystery of the Cantern was currently at the top of my attention priority list.

Edgar reached out and touched the tree's trunk, and as we watched a panel opened, revealing a chamber within. And there, sitting on a small pedestal, was …

"*That's* the Cantern?" I asked.

On the pedestal was a wooden stick, about a foot long. It was a dark walnut color, and it seemed old and antique. It had what looked like a handle at one end, with a pommel of sorts — a knot of wood encircled by three concentric metal rings. It tapered to a conical point at the other end. Spiraling around the length of it it was an engraved woven pattern that I quickly confirmed was entwined with the knotwork. This thing was *Teth*.

Edgar gingerly took the wooden object out of the tree and turned to face us, holding it in front of him.

"Go ahead," Xander said. "Take it."

"Me? Why me?" I asked.

"I can't touch it," Xander said. "It could have … side effects. But you're a *Teth*. You'll be fine."

I looked from Xander to the object, then nodded and reached out. Edgar leaned slightly forward, handing it to me, and then straightening back up.

I felt the weight of it in my hands, and looked at it appreciatively. It was somewhat heavy for its size. Other than the carved pattern that encircled it end-to-end, it had no markings or anything to identify what it was for. "Thanks," I said to Edgar, and gave a slight bow of my head. I wasn't sure if that was what was required, but it felt right.

"Put it in your bag," Xander said.

"Is it a wand or something?" I asked.

"Who are you, Harry Potter?" Xander asked. "No, it's not a wand. It's a spool."

"A spool? Like a sewing spool?"

"More like a bobbin, like a spool you'd put on a large machine, for sewing or weaving. That's what they used to look like, back in the day," Xander said, nodding to it.

"What day, exactly?"

"Days before your days. Now put it in the bag."

I did this, and then closed the flap of the bag again. "Ok. Now what?" I asked.

Xander shrugged. "Now we eat." He looked at Edgar. "You've made beef stew, I'm sure."

There was a strange sound from Edgar, which I eventually interpreted as light laughter.

Xander looked at me, "He's a strict vegetarian. I told him a joke."

"He's a vegetarian? He eats?"

"Don't all living things eat?" Xander asked.

I had no ready answer for that.

We followed Edgar through the woods once again, until we came to a table and chairs, just sitting amidst the trees and underbrush. There was a campfire nearby, and hanging from a tripod was a large pot. Its contents were simmering a bit. I could smell what was cooking, though I couldn't place it.

Edgar motioned for us to sit, which we did. 8-Ball hovered past us, disappearing into the brush. I started to ask where he was going, but instead watched as Edgar dished ladles of his soup into bowls, handing one to each of us.

Xander smiled, raised his bowl as if toasting with it, and then sipped it noisily. No need for a spoon.

I followed his lead, though I was a bit quieter.

The soup was a vegetable broth, and it was incredibly tasty. It had a thickness to it that was filling all on its own, and the vegetables were tender and delicious. It was the best soup I'd ever had.

Xander smacked his lips and set his bowl down, now only about half full. "Outstanding as always, Edgar!" he said.

Edgar was taking his own seat, and was sipping soup from his bowl, raising it mechanically to metal lips, tilting it *just so*, then tilting it back. It was strange to watch.

He was quiet, but not unresponsive. I could sense that he was pleased with Xander's compliment, and with our company. I wondered how long he'd been alone here.

As he ate, I was again struck by how *human* he seemed. And why not? He *was* human, although a human in a twisted form. I looked at his knotwork, and again felt a sort of revulsion. Seeing what the wizard had done to this man was too much. It was horrible. A nightmare.

As Edgar quietly enjoyed his soup, and Xander chatted on amicably, I began to feel my way around Edgar's knotwork, in much the way I had with my own knotwork earlier. If Gram had tried and failed to undo the damage, it must be pretty serious. Those loose threads had to be bad news, for starters. And the "bruising" just looked flat-out painful.

On a whim, I mentally reached out, brushing the loose threads with that part of my mind that seemed able to do such things. I was only just starting to get an understanding of how this worked. Or maybe "understanding" was too strong of a word. I was starting to get a *feel* for it, at least.

As I brushed the threads, I felt the overall pattern. Not the pattern that was, but the pattern that *used to be*. The pattern that *should* be. It was still there, mangled out of shape by the wizard's manipulation, but still intact enough for me to get the sense of it.

What if I could retie those threads?

On a whim, I began experimenting, exploring the torn and loose threads to see which should fit together, and where they lead.

I started with the loose ones, but quickly found that I would have to follow the lines deeper into Edgar's twisted knotwork. Doing this felt weird, sort of like having a stomach ache and a headache all at once. It was light at first, but became worse as I went further in.

Because that's exactly what I was doing. On instinct, I was going deeper and deeper into the knotwork, carrying the loose threads with me. I was following old trails, which had not been followed in thousands of years, and pushing through a sort of knotwork "underbrush" that didn't belong there.

It was then that I realized I was stuck.

Somehow, in following Edgar's knotwork, I had managed to tangle my own into the twisted snarls and snags left by that wizard who would be a god. I struggled, at first, to pull myself free, but that just seemed to tangle me more. After a few seconds of this, I decided instead that the only way out was *through*.

I worked deeper into the knotwork, and as I did I reconnected severed threads, loosened and unlooped old knots, and straightened spirals of thread that should have never been twisted together. I could see it all — the pattern that was and the pattern that *should be*. It was a mess, and the story was disjointed and wrong in so many ways, but as I worked I could see more and more of what the pattern was meant to be.

The deeper I went, though, the more entangled I became, and the more determined I was to unravel it all and set it right.

It took a great deal of time. I wasn't sure how long, but I knew that a lot of time was passing. I kept at it. I had no choice. At this point, I would either have to figure this out, and untangle and retie the whole mess, or give up and remain trapped as part of it. I couldn't go back, and I could only go forward by *fixing* it.

I was making progress. The paths were becoming straighter, the knots cleaner and more natural. The story that was supposed to be told was suddenly becoming clear. And as I worked out the kinks and twists and snares that didn't belong, I found myself suddenly through the whole thing, and free once again.

I gasped, and sat up, panting. Xander was leaning over me, and 8-Ball was hovering nearby. Xander looked incredibly concerned. "You idiot!" he said. "Didn't you hear me tell you how dangerous that was going to be?"

"I ..." I panted, and I suddenly felt very heavy, and more than a little tired. "Sorry," I said, settling back again, laying flat on the floor.

Xander looked as if he were about to say something else, then shook his head, and finally smiled. "Sorry? I think you have nothing to apologize for, Sawyer. In fact, I think someone wants to have a word with you."

I was too tired to sit up again, but I did manage to turn my head in the direction Xander was nodding. Standing there, with a look of wonder on his face, was a strange man. He looked at me, and smiled, tears streaming down his cheeks. "Thank you," he said, his voice a hoarse whisper. "Thank you, thank you, thank you!"

I blinked. "Who?" I asked.

Xander laughed. "You really are an idiot. Sawyer Jackson, meet Edgar. Formerly an automaton. Now human again, thanks to you. So much for the impossible!"

I smiled then, as much as a I could, before passing out entirely.

SEVEN | NOGOODNIKS

I woke up in a large bed in the middle of the faux woods. I was fully dressed, except for my boots and the button-up overshirt I'd been wearing. The "sky" overhead was mostly dark, and toward the horizon it was a dozen shades of red. Sunset, I figured. I must have been out for a long time — it had been morning when we entered the building and started winding our way down here..

I slipped out of bed and found my boots on the ground. My shirt was hanging from the bed post. I pulled on both, buttoning the shirt and rolling up the sleeves. Looking around, I could see that the bed was in a sort of clearing, surrounded by dozens of trees that stood close enough to each other to make walls of a sort. It was like being in a room with no ceiling, except there *was* a ceiling. And I really was in a room. And it was all very confusing when you started looking at it too closely.

I heard talking from one direction, low and murmuring, and made my way toward it. The wall of trees thinned in that direction, and underbrush and leafy vines made a sort of door that I could pass through easy enough.

"What of the others?" a voice asked from further ahead, through the brush. It sounded like Edgar, though it was less "mechanical" than before.

Xander's voice answered. "If he can help, I'm sure he will. He's a good kid. But you saw how much it took out of him. It's dangerous.

He has enough danger in his life right now. I have to get him and the Cantern out of this Layer. We'll need to keep moving for a bit."

I was closing in on them when 8-Ball came floating in front of me. I stopped, and it shook itself in mid-air. When I looked at the little window it read, " Don't count on it."

I blinked. "Don't …"

8-Ball zipped forward, stopping just short of smacking me in the face. I flinched back, nearly falling to the ground.

8-Ball shook itself, and in the window I saw that the little message block was a bit tilted, rather than settling flat against the window. Now it read, "Don't," which faded off slightly in the murky blue water.

Don't what? Don't leave? Don't speak? Don't interrupt Xander and Edgar?

"Where will you go?" Edgar asked.

"Many places, I'm sure!" Xander exclaimed.

Edgar sighed. "You do not trust me," he said.

Xander chuckled, "No, Edgar. But don't take it personally. I have thousands of years of paranoia built up. Trust isn't something I do often."

"What of the event? Have you determined what it will be? Will Sawyer be prepared?"

"I don't know," Xander said. "I believe I've at least narrowed down the Layer where the event will take place. Whether Sawyer will be prepared is more or less up to him. His grandparents taught him very well. He's smart, and he doesn't rattle easily. And he's brave to the point of being an idiot."

I rankled a bit at that one.

"His actions were perhaps foolish, but I am eternally in his debt," Edgar said.

"I think we'll all be eternally in his debt, by the time it's all said and done."

8-Ball suddenly shook itself again, and in the little window I read, "Outlook good."

I took this to mean it was ok to go to Xander and Edgar now, and I did.

They were seated on large stones around a small fire. The fire wasn't real, though it looked realistic enough. I could see that it was some sort of light play — maybe a holographic projection. That made sense. You wouldn't want a *real* campfire burning indoors.

They looked up as I approached. 8-Ball floated on ahead of me, hovering around a large stone where I eventually took a seat.

"Sleep well?" Xander asked.

I yawned. "I think so," I said. "Looks like I was out for a while. Sun's going down."

Xander laughed. "Coming up, actually."

I blinked. "Coming up? How long was I out?"

Xander checked his wrist, which did not have a wristwatch on it. "Maybe 18 hours. Ish."

"Eighteen hours!"

Xander smiled. "Could have been a lot longer. As in permanent. I have never seen a *Teth* do what you did yesterday. Pretty impressive. Don't do it again without giving some warning first, got it?"

I shook my head, feeling the weariness still clinging to my brain. "I'm not even sure what I did. I just sort of followed the knotwork."

"You freed me from thousands of years of enslavement to an evil tyrant who would be a god!" Edgar said suddenly. He was excited — or at least, his voice sounded excited. He was nearly motionless as he talked. Must have been a long-formed habit. "I cannot thank you enough, Sawyer Jackson." And now I noticed the streams of tears running down his cheek, catching bits of firelight. He was shaking, as if his emotions, trapped within him for thousands of years, were finally breaking to the surface.

I smiled as best I could. "You're welcome, Edgar. I'm happy I could help. I'm sorry you suffered that way for so long."

Edgar nodded, overtaken by emotion, I supposed.

"Fixing Edgar was impressive enough," Xander said. "But what really got me was the fact that you didn't even move. Most *Teth* have to at least have to create some kind of pattern, with string or a drawing or something. At the very least they have to make patterns in the air as they reach into the knotwork. You were just *looking* at him. How did you do it?"

I shook my head. "I'm not sure. I just ... *did it*. Sort of followed the loose threads that were hanging from Edgar, and moved into the knotwork, sort of like swimming into a tunnel. I got tangled, actually. My knotwork was caught up in the snags and tears in Edgar's knotwork. I was pretty stuck for a while."

Xander nodded. "Your Gram said that to change Edgar's patten would require a *Teth* to become entangled within it. She told me the odds of Edgar surviving that entanglement were zero. And the odds for the *Teth* were pretty slim, too."

My eyes widened. "Zero? You mean ... I could have killed Edgar?"

Xander leaned forward, looking me in the eye. His expression, usually genial and even a little goofy, was hard set and stern. "Yes," he said. "You could have. That's what makes this gift of yours so dangerous, Sawyer. And that's why I want you to tell me before you try anything like that again. Losing Edgar would have been sad. He's a good man, and a good friend. But losing you might cost the Omni in ways I can't even calculate. And I can calculate to a lot of decimal places."

I thought about this for a while, then nodded. "Yeah, ok. I'm sorry. I didn't realize. I didn't know I could do that myself. I just ... it was instinct."

Xander continued looking at me, intense and hard, for another few seconds, as if peering into my brain to study me. And then he relented, leaned back, smiled. "I know," he said. "That's what made it so *cool*. And it's very encouraging, this instinct of yours to do good. Gives me hope."

I thought about this. I was glad for that instinct, too. But there was still that nagging part of me that wondered about people like the "god" who had turned Edgar into an automaton, or Aeodymus, who was so evil that Xander and the others had been forced to use an entire universe as his prison. The wizards that Gram and Gramps and Xander seemed to despise were all *Teth*, all gifted with the same abilities I had. Powerful. Maybe with a natural talent. Just like me.

What made them turn? Would the same thing happen to me?

As I sat, brooding and watching the fire, the sky gradually lightened and shifted from shades of red to a crystal blue. The air seemed cool, but not uncomfortable. The sound of birds made everything feel surreal but inviting. I could see why Edgar chose to stay here. Given how *unnatural* his life had become, living in this place must have been the closest he could come to being human. I wasn't sure what this world was like, outside of this building. Xander had said they understood that technology could be a part of the living world. Still, Edgar would be a constant reminder of an ancient and dark time. And he had to be something of a spectacle, in the outside world. He had chosen to live alone, in these artificial woods, rather than out among other humans. There would be a reason for that.

Edgar brought me a bowl of something to eat. It was sort of like oatmeal, only a finer grain. It was thick and warm, with a slightly sweet flavor. And it was very filling. I ate it and sipped a cup of coffee that was better than anything I'd ever gotten at any Starbucks anywhere.

"We're going to have to get moving," Xander said. "This Layer is pretty well protected against incursions from the Inks or other minions Aeodymus might employ. But it's not impenetrable. There are ticks everywhere, scouting."

I sipped more coffee, and asked, "Where do we go from here?"

Xander thought about this for a while. "I have a couple of holes to patch. Many holes, actually, but there is one that needs more immediate attention. Unfortunately, it's a Layer where a lot of corrupt *Teth* or other nogoodniks might be hanging out."

"Nogoodniks?"

"Ne'er-do-wells," Xander said.

I shook my head.

"Bad guys?"

"Gotcha," I said.

"Pardon," Edgar said. "But if the Layer is full of 'nogoodniks,' why must you go there?"

Xander sighed. "There are a couple of reasons. The first is that there's a particularly nasty tear there, and one that needs to be stitched up before it gets worse. But the other reason is 8-Ball."

I looked at 8-Ball, who was floating near me. "Did he tell you to take me there?" I asked.

"Not directly, but in his way, yes," Xander said, a sour expression on his face.

That was good enough for me. I understood why Xander was so frustrated with the "Akashic Sphere." The cryptic answers and insistent silence made it impossible to know its motivations or intentions. But I had a theory building. If 8-Ball was the sum total of all knowledge in the Omni — past, present, and potential future — then it had a vested interest in keeping the Omni safe. Which, I was sure, was exactly why Xander tolerated having him along. We all had a common interest and a common enemy. 8-Ball was the only one who would know exactly how all this might play out, and which pieces on the board were most important.

The silence bugged me, but I knew that was my own issue. 8-Ball limited the information it shared because too much information can be dangerous. Knowing what's coming might influence the choices we made in a way that did more damage than simply letting things happen. And knowing too much about the *present*, about what was going on in other Layers or even with Aeodymus — that might cause us to refuse to act at all. There was a balance at play here. 8-Ball was hovering along a fine line just by being with us.

"Well, if 8-Ball says we should go, then we should probably get going," I said.

Xander smiled, and placed his coffee mug on a wooden stump that served as a sort of side table. "Edgar, it's been brilliant as always. Thank you for your hospitality."

"You are always welcome here," Edgar said. He was facing me, still as a stone, staring.

"Um, thanks," I said. "I'm really glad you're ok, Edgar. I'm … I'm sorry I almost killed you."

"I would gladly risk a thousand deaths for the gift you have given me," Edgar said.

"What will you do now that you're human again?" Xander asked.

Edgar looked at Xander, and I could see a sort of uneasy, long unpracticed smile on his face. "I will stay here, for a time. Other humans come here, on occasion. As do the other remaining automatons. I will tell them of Sawyer Jackson. And we will live in hope of his eventual return to our Layer."

I exchanged glances with Xander, who gave me a cautious look. I turned back to Edgar, "How many automatons are there now?" I asked.

"There are three remaining. The others perished long ago, in various ways."

Three more. Could I change three more people, the way I changed Edgar? It was a huge risk, for them and for me. What if the first time was a fluke? What if I couldn't figure out how to do it again? "One day, Edgar, I'll come back here, if I can. But I want you to tell the others about the risks of this. It could kill them. It could also just fail to work altogether. Or I could die trying it. I want to learn more about what I can do, and how I do it. And when I'm sure I can help without hurting, I'll come back."

Edgar nodded. "That is all we can ask. The automatons are nothing if not patient."

Xander also nodded, apparently approving of my plan and commitment.

We gathered our things, and Edgar supplied us with a few provisions for the road, including a small bag of coffee that I coveted.

After saying our goodbyes, Xander reached into the lining of his coat, plucked a button free, and used it to open reality so we could step through and into another Layer of the Omniverse.

We walked very slowly and cautiously along the path, which hugged a wall of natural stone on one side and dropped into oblivion on the other. We'd been walking this way for a couple of hours, each step pretty measured before moving on.

Xander had tied us together with a long rope before we started. "I got this from a *Teth* I knew around the same time I met your Gram. They created a pattern in the knotwork that makes the rope coil up and retract like a spring if you pull the two ends apart from each other at high speed. Handy for zipping you back up the side of a mountain, if you fall."

"Or yanking someone else down with you," I said.

"Don't be negative," Xander replied with a scowl.

We plodded on up the winding mountain path, only stopping occasionally to drink from our canteens or nibble on a few provisions. These were the moments where I could concentrate on the scenery. A valley stretched out for miles in every direction, dotted with small villages and woven with winding roads. We were high enough that clouds sometimes blocked part of the view, but that just made it all the more breathtaking.

At one stop, I looked around, alarmed. "Where's 8-Ball?" I asked.

Xander chuckled. "He does that. Just disappears. Sometimes he's gone for days. It's his prerogative, of course. I gave up long ago on trying to tell him what to do, or even trying to figure out what he was thinking. He's the Akashic Sphere — if he wants to go bounce along on the Layers without me, he's going to do it."

I nodded, though I felt a little unsettled. I'd come to like 8-Ball, though I barely knew him. I knew he had an agenda, which was understandable. But he seemed friendly, even helpful. He was quiet, but somehow had a loud presence when he needed to. It was comforting, having him around. Of course, even now, I felt that maybe he was nearby. He *did* know everything there was to know, after all. I supposed he knew exactly where we were and even what I was thinking. In a way, he'd always be watching.

As we leaned against the wall, as far from the edge as we could get while resting, I looked out over the valley that stretched before us, and was reminded of another mountain I'd been on recently.

"Xander, tell me a little about the Long Land. I've only seen a small part of it. The Cabin was interesting but pretty isolated. And the other time I was there was on accident. I landed on top of a mountain."

Xander nodded, sipping from his canteen. "Your people sure like to put tears on top of mountains." He waved the canteen up the path. "Case in point."

"Why?" I asked.

He shook his head. "Reasons vary. The Layers can be tough to penetrate sometimes. The more activity a certain spot has, the stronger the threads in that area. A powerful *Teth* can get through the weave of the place, but it can be uncomfortable. Mountains, deserts, ice caps — these are remote places, where the knotwork has more gaps. Makes it easier to come through. Especially if they don't know exactly where they're going."

"So is it always a tear? When a *Teth* travels, does it always damage the Layer?"

Xander shook his head. "No, not at all. A skilled *Teth* can open the weave a bit and slip through, then close it behind. That's the right way. Some don't bother. Some can't do it because they lack the skill, or the patience. Some actually *want* to tear the fabric of reality."

"Why?" I asked. "Doesn't that just cause problems?"

"Of course," Xander said quietly. "But it also creates power. The corrupt *Teth* who become wizards or gods or conquerors, they do what they do by manipulating the threads of the knotwork. And torn threads let them reshape reality any way they want. Just like you did with Edgar."

"I didn't know what I was doing exactly," I said.

He eyed me. "Oh, I know," he said. "It was pretty stupid."

I felt my face flush and a small pressure build in my temples. "I don't know that 'stupid' is the word I'd use," I said, my words clipped and tight. "I'd be willing to accept 'ignorant.'"

Xander smiled and shook his head. "Just like your Gram. Your bloodline is pretty hung up on words and meaning. I think it's the storytelling aspect of your abilities."

I thought about this. "You know, when I'm looking at the knotwork, I am sort of 'reading' it, like a story. It talks to me, in a way. It tells me about itself, and what it means."

Xander regarded me for a moment and said, "A rare gift."

"Can't all *Teth* do that?"

He shook his head. "No, not even close. Your Gram does it, though I don't think she's quite as talented with it as you appear to be."

For some reason this gave me a little thrill. Gram and Gramps were my benchmark for all things brilliant and capable. To know that I might be able to do something better than Gram, something we both shared in common, was kind of cool. It was also a little scary. I had Gramps in my head saying, "Don't get cocky. Everyone has their strengths and their weaknesses. Just because you haven't spotted your weakness doesn't mean you don't have one." He'd said that to me after I beat him at chess a dozen times in a row. I'd sort of laughed about it then, but now I was thinking he might have been trying to teach me and prepare me for here and now. He had to have known that something like this was coming, someday.

Thinking of Gram and Gramps made me feel homesick. I missed them so much. It had been several days since we'd left them at the cabin, and so much had happened that I wanted to share with them, or ask them about.

To distract myself, I asked Xander more questions.

"When I was on that mountain, I saw that the Long Land really is some kind of strip. I don't know how wide, though. It has oceans on either side?"

"Two oceans, divided by a single strip of land that encircles the globe. Just the one continent. It's maybe three thousand miles wide all the way around."

'Three thousand! There's no way I could have seen three thousand miles from that height. I was able to make out details, like forests and rivers."

Xander laughed. "I forget you're pretty new at this. When you landed on that mountain, you were standing in a small tear or open weave in the fabric of reality. There's a sort of distortion that can happen in spots like that. The *Teth* have a natural ability to see and interpret reality at a deeper level than anyone else, so you were probably doing some things on instinct when you landed there. Given the vantage point, the distortion, and your pretty substantial gift with the knotwork, I'm pretty sure you weren't really 'there,' but were sort of in-between. What you saw was a translation, of a sort."

I struggled with this. "Like looking through the bottom of a glass? You get a sort of magnification, but also some distortion."

Xander smiled. "Sounds about right."

I nodded. "Ok, I think I have it." I stared out over the landscape again. I was feeling rested, and I knew that any moment we'd be moving again. We'd avoid talking, so we could concentrate on the narrow path. So if I had any pressing questions, I needed to ask them now.

"Xander … what does Aeodymus want with me?"

Xander was also looking out over the landscape. He closed his canteen and stowed it in his bag, then picked up a small stone and chucked it out and over the edge. I watched it fall away, wondering for a second about where it might end up — a small stone from the side of a mountain, now cast out into the open air, hurtling toward a spot where it would likely stay forever, unless some traveler picked it up or it got caught in the tread of a shoe or otherwise just had *life* happen to it.

"He doesn't want anything *with* you," Xander replied, finally. "He wants to *use* you to break free of the Layer where I trapped him."

"How?" I asked.

Xander shook his head. "He has his plans. None of them are good, for you or for the Omni. If he escapes that Layer, he's going to do a lot of damage. He'll shred the knotwork and remake everything in his own image, if he's given the chance."

"Is he that powerful?" I asked.

"You're *all* that powerful," Xander said. "With the right motivation." He looked at me, hard, and asked, "Do you know why more *Teth* don't become like Aeodymus?"

I shook my head.

"Some of it is natural ability and talent. Most *Teth* are nowhere near as skilled as you or your Gram. Those that are — sometimes they let the power corrupt them. They ignore the responsibility of their abilities and go on a power grab, ripping reality to literal shreds and tying it back together to suit them. That's how Aeodymus started. They set themselves up as rulers and gods. For some, ruling a nation or even a world is enough. For others, like Aeodymus, there's *never* enough. They can't live with the story of the Omni. They want to change it until it's *their* story. But for most of the corrupt *Teth*, the thing that blocks them from gaining ultimate power is the risk of losing their own story, and becoming hopelessly entangled in the knotwork. It's happened before. Some of the tears in reality that I've repaired over the eons were actually snarls in the knotwork created by trapped *Teth*."

He looked at me, I guess to see if all of this was registering. It was. I thought about Edgar and the tangle of his knotwork, how it caught me up when I was trying to fix it. I could see the danger in that.

Xander stood up from his crouched position against the wall, dusted himself off, threw his bag over his shoulder, and said, "Time to get moving. We're close. Another hour or so, I think."

I nodded and slung my own bag across my chest. Xander started walking, and I started thinking. It was dangerous to let my mind wander too much, on this narrow trail up the side of a sheer cliff. But as we got into the rhythm of the walk, and as Xander was guiding us carefully up the mountainside, I found I had plenty of mental bandwidth to go on autopilot and daydream.

So far I'd more or less operated by instinct, when it came to the knotwork. I was getting better at what I was doing, but I can't say that I was learning in great strides. I needed direction and guidance. Without it, I was going to end up blundering into trouble, like I almost had with Edgar.

Without Gram, I wasn't sure how I'd learn. Xander wasn't a *Teth*, though he was pretty knowledgeable, after thousands of years. But he couldn't give me the particulars. Just the warnings and cautions.

If only there was some kind of Google for the *Teth* and the Long Land and the Layers.

This jarred me. *Maybe there is*, I thought.

I reached into my shirt as we walked, and pulled out the woven necklace Gram had made for me. I looked at it — really *looked*, deep into its knotwork — and there it was, shining bright like a star, with billions of tiny threads spiraling out of it.

The braid.

Gram had told me it was a sort of history of the bloodline. As I looked, I could see just how true that was. All those spiraling patterns were connected to the lives of generations of my own bloodline, weaving backward through time.

I let the necklace fall to my chest. I didn't have to look at it directly to follow the patterns in the braid. I could do like I'd done with Edgar, and sort of mentally follow the knotwork.

I did this cautiously. Unlike with Edgar, I wasn't trying to unravel or re-tie the knotwork of the braid. Instead, I was following it the way your eye follows text on a page. I scanned it for meaning, let the story of it carry me, let the details come.

It happened slowly, but as we plodded on it became easier to sift through all the data I was reading. I found that if I wanted to find something specific, I could "search" for it by imagining the story I needed, in as much detail as I was able, and letting it click and fit naturally within the knotwork. This worked well — the bits of the story I imagined and got "right" naturally fit with what was in the braid, and connected to the rest of the story, and I started to see the overall pattern come alive.

As I went, the story I wove picked up details and gained in complexity. One twist would match something within the knotwork — generally some bit of the story I already knew. From there, I'd discover another small pattern, and fold that in. I did this, on and on, until a full pattern began to emerge.

It was there.

All the knowledge of all the *Teth* in my bloodline was right there, ready for me to read. I would have to *study* it, to learn from what I was seeing. It wasn't like installing some kind of library in my head. I would have to do the work of reading it, interpreting, digging for details. But I could *see it*, whole and complex and beautiful, stretching out in every direction.

I could learn to do this. All I had to do was spend the time and ask the right questions. It would be a long process, nudging information and training out of the pattern. But as I experimented and tried things out, I noticed my own pattern, and how it was growing in complexity as well. The learning would happen. I could guide it and nurture it.

While I was engrossed in studying the braid, Xander stopped and waited for me to catch up.

We were on a plateau of sorts. It was a large, flat area that dug into the side of the mountain, which continued to rise up for miles into the sky. There was an overhang of rock that formed a sort of roof, and where it curved down to meet the ground there was a small, ragged looking opening to a cave.

Or, at least, I *thought* it was a cave. As I looked closer I could see that it wasn't cut into the mountain as much as it was *punched* through it — and everything else in this reality.

"There it is," Xander said. "The tear."

I looked at its knotwork. Sure enough, it resembled a piece of ripped fabric, with threads hanging loose, moving as if in a light breeze. Around it's edges, the threads looked strained and bruised. I was starting to realize just how *alive* the knotwork was, and how much damage these tears could cause.

"What do we do?" I asked. "Just go up and start tying it back together?"

Xander shook his head. "Stay still. There's no telling what's on the other side of that tear. It may not even go to another Layer."

"Where would it go?" I asked.

"The In-Between," Xander said.

"The what now?"

He turned to me, "There's a space between multiverses. It's what keeps the clusters from interacting with each other. Every universe in a multiverse is an alternate. Universes in different multiverses are parallels. That's necessary for the Omniverse to be what it is. So, by necessity, there's a space between multiverses."

"Ok," I said. "And that's clearly not a good place, judging by your reaction."

Xander shook his head. "I'm not sure if you can call it good or bad. It just *is*. Or *isn't*, depending on your point of view. The things that live in the In-Between can be pretty vicious, though. They've had a hard life."

Suddenly we heard a screaming, screeching sound from the tear. It was like hearing two pieces of heavy metal wreckage being wrenched apart. It was sort of hollow and resonating, and it lingered long after it faded.

"Uh oh," Xander said.

"I don't even know what that was and I agree," I said.

He turned to me, and untied the rope from around his waist as he talked. I did the same. "You go nowhere near that tear unless I tell you to," Xander said.

I nodded.

"And if anything comes out, you run and hide."

Again, I nodded. "What are you going to do?" I asked.

"Avoid dying," he said, then smiled.

"I thought you couldn't die?"

He looked at me as if I were insane. "Of course I can die. Where'd you get that idea?"

"Aren't you, like, older than everything or something?"

"I'm alive, which means I can die. That's what being alive *means*, Sawyer. Now, you concentrate on staying that way as well." He rolled up the rope as he walked away, stowing it in his bag. In the process he pulled out a long, rust-colored metal rod that could not possibly have been in there if it were a normal bag.

The rod looked to be made of iron, though Xander carried it as if it weighed nothing. It was about six foot long, and even from this distance I could see that it had hundreds of raised markings on it. Looking at it through the knotwork, I could see some pretty exotic twists and turns. The story of this thing was one of speed and battering. It told of being lightweight while in the hand, but also infinitely heavy on impact.

It was a weapon. An iron staff. And Xander wielded it like a pro, spinning it and grasping it in an expert grip.

The screeching sound returned, and as I watched *something* came out of the tear in reality.

It had a long body, like a snake, coiling and zagging out of the tear and onto the plateau. Its head was narrow and cone-shaped, ending in a strange-looking mouth at its tip, which was filled with sharp-looking spikes. From the back of its head was a mane of spines — thousands of them shot back from the head like porcupine quills, ending in dangerous-looking points. The creature's eyes were large and almond shaped. They were bright green, mottled with flecks of black. The pupils were horizontal slits that narrowed as the creature came into the light.

Once it was through the tear, it coiled nearby, and looked around. Spotting Xander, it became rigid, and began to split down the middle, as if its body was some kind of carapace. Emerging from this were two long, spindly legs that ended in what looked like horse hooves. A set of long and wiry arms curled outward as well, terminating in needle-like claws on far too many fingers. The carapace continued to fold backward until it resembled two narrow wings on the creature's back.

It hunched and faced off with Xander, who was expertly spinning the iron rod, taking a fighting stance that put the rod between him and the creature.

I looked at the thing's knotwork, and was repelled. Instead of the healthy amber glow of the living knotwork I was used to, this thing had twists of black and oozing twine. It had a sort of degraded integrity — tendrils of broken threads curled off of it in a way that reminded me of a decaying animal corpse. Coarse, oily, black and disgusting — this thing was in no way part of the Omni.

It screeched again, and I felt my guts twist. I wanted to vomit at the sound of it. I could only imagine what Xander was experiencing, up close.

Xander started methodically stepping sideways, keeping the iron staff at the ready and keeping his eyes on the creature at all times. He maneuvered it so that his back was to the outer edge of the plateau, an expanse of open air stretching for miles in every direction. The creature was between him and the tear, and from my vantage point it seemed Xander was trying to keep it there.

He's trying to get it to go back, I thought.

It was a sort of revelation, that Xander wasn't actually trying to *kill* this thing. I looked at his knotwork, which was vast and complex and brighter than any living knotwork I'd seen so far, short of 8-Ball's. I could see, on the surface-most level of his story that he was trying to persuade this thing to go home, and that he didn't want to kill it if he could avoid it.

But he *would* kill it, rather than let it loose on this Layer. That was clear, too.

The thing raised up on its hind hooves, and took several quick swipes with its clawed hands. Xander dodged one and deflected the other with the staff, which caused sparks to rain down. Xander swung the staff in a wide arc, which the creature dodged by stepping backward, toward the tear.

Xander pressed his advantage, spinning the staff in front of him, occasionally jabbing one end at the creature, which screamed loud and high enough to shatter glass.

Suddenly the thing leapt forward, swatting the staff aside and taking another swipe at Xander, the needles of its claws catching the front of Xander's shirt. The fabric tore away in shreds.

"Yah!" Xander cried, again swinging the rod. This time it made contact with the thing's head, and the blow made the creature stagger back, temporarily dazed.

It recovered before Xander could press his advantage, and this time when it screamed the small mouth retracted, widening as it went. It opened into a large circle of needle teeth, in multiple rows that spiraled back into the creature's head. Its jaws opened wide, and now it looked as if its head was composed entirely of teeth.

It was *mad*.

Xander stepped back and raised the staff like a spear. I saw him whisper something to it, which I couldn't hear. But in the knotwork I saw a flash of light, and a tendril wove itself outward, connecting the staff to the creature.

Xander took a quick step forward and hurled the staff, which spiraled along the thread until it slammed into the creature's mouth, snapping hundreds of the needle teeth as it went. The thing's head snapped back, and its momentum carried it over, head-first, into the tear.

More than momentum, though. It kept sliding backward, even after it hit the ground. It was being *pushed* through the tear by the rod!

Xander, his arm still extended after the throw and his palm out, was somehow pushing the creature into the tear, using the staff. When the last of it went through, he made a grasping gesture, pulling back, and the rod emerged from the tear, sailing back into his hands.

Xander rushed forward, reaching into the lining of his coat and pulling a button free. He also reached into one pocket and pulled out something that looked exactly like the Cantern. It was wound with thread.

"Little help?" Xander called over his shoulder.

I rushed forward as Xander started making sewing motions in the air, pulling thread from the bobbin as he went. For the first time I noticed that he was holding a small needle, which was tied to the thread.

As he pulled the thread tighter, the tear in reality began to close. He glanced at me. "I know this is your first time, but this tear was worse than I thought. Can you take a look at the knotwork? Maybe give it a nudge? Tie it to this thread," he said.

I looked at the knotwork around the tear and saw the loose threads. He was doing a fair job of closing the hole, but it wasn't a perfect seam. I reached out, mentally, and started gathering the loose ends, tying them together into a story that included the thread. This would be a scar in the knotwork, I could see. But a scar is better than an open wound.

The hole was slowly closing, and it looked like we were in the clear. Which, of course, meant that we weren't.

Suddenly we heard the screeching sound again, and a spiked hand shot out of the hole, which was smaller now but still not closed.

Xander and I fell backward, trying to avoid the swishing of the the razor-sharp claws. Xander got to his feet first, picked up the rod, and used it like a baseball bat to strike the hand again and again. It refused to budge.

Looking at it in the knotwork, I could see that all of this was starting to tear the seam back open. If we didn't get this thing under control soon it would tear its way back into this world.

I reached out again, mentally grabbing all the loose threads. This time I looped them outward, forming a cage of threads around the creature's hand. I tightened this, and heard the thing scream.

Xander took advantage of the moment. He gripped the staff in both hands and pressed its length against the flailing hand. He pushed, and as he did I made the threads pull. In a moment, the hand was forced back through the hole. I quickly wove the threads into a net, closing the hole as best I could. Xander did the rest, running his thread in and out of the tear, cinching it closed at the end. Then, in a rush, he stood and held up the button between this thumb and forefinger. He eyed the last remaining bit of tear, and with a quick motion struck with the button, using it to fasten the tear closed. There was a flash, and as I watched the seam disappeared from normal view. I could still see it there, a purple scar in the knotwork. But for anyone else standing by, it was invisible. It never existed.

Xander and I collapsed onto the ground nearby, huffing.

"That … " I started.

Xander held up a hand, halting me. "Not normal," he said. "Yeah. I know."

EIGHT | THINGS AREN'T NORMAL

We moved from Layer to Layer in quick bursts. In some cases, we'd no sooner land in a layer than Xander would snap a button from the inside of his coat and we'd be off to the next.

"Is there a reason we're burning through the Layers like a couple of lunatics?" I asked, huffing and out of breath. We'd just made at least six jumps without stopping.

"Leaving breadcrumbs," Xander said.

"Breadcrumbs?"

He glanced at me as he pulled another button loose and opened a seam in reality. We stepped through and he "did it up," closing it tight and letting the burned out button fall as ash to the ground. "That thing we fought on the mountain — it wasn't something I was expecting."

"You knew something might come out of that tear, right? You said that happens. That's why you're closing those tears, isn't it?"

He nodded. "I expected *something* to come out of that hole, but not what came out. It took me a while to recognize it. It wasn't until it had completely unfurled itself that I knew. That was a Quill. One of the creatures Aeodymus created."

"A Quill? Ok, wait … are all of the things Aeodymus created named after Victorian writing tools?"

Xander chuckled. "Not all. But you have to remember that Aeodymus is old. Not as old as me, but pretty old compared to you. His sensibilities are from a different time. Most of the creatures he created have been around for quite awhile."

"That thing … when I looked at it, I could see that its knotwork was wrong somehow. Bruised looking. Black and nasty."

Xander nodded. We had stopped on this Layer, and after he closed the portal we walked at a nice, leisurely pace down a city sidewalk. I was grateful to slow down. It was a little exhausting, moving from one reality to another in rapid succession. There was a sort of acclimation that had to happen, I discovered. Kind of like letting your ears pop on an airplane. Moving as fast as we were, I wasn't getting that. I felt uncomfortable, maybe a little sick to my stomach.

In the current Layer we were in what looked like a typical town center. It could have been Earth Prime for all I knew. There were shops lining a main street, selling things that seemed familiar. Clothes were the primary thing I saw in shop windows, but there were also stores that sold cooking utensils, learning toys, and candles. I looked for a book store — that might have told me a bit more about the place, but it also would have been nice to browse some shelves, if we could. I missed book stores.

We strolled until we came to a cafe. Xander asked the waiter for two mineral waters with lime. I wasn't much of a fan of mineral water, but I'd drink just about anything at that moment, I realized. When they came, I gulped mine down.

"I had no idea I was so thirsty," I said.

"Moving between layers can take a lot out of you. Rest. Refresh. We'll need to get going again soon."

I sucked on one of the ice cubes for a bit. The waiter brought a refill, and this time I sipped a bit slower.

"Why are we running?" I asked.

"The presence of the Quill means that factions aligned with

Aeodymus have found a way to track us," Xander said. "I'm not sure how, yet. But I suspect he's found a way to see my button holes in the universe. None of his disgusting little beasts have come for us directly, though, so I'm gambling that he can't target us specifically. The presence of a tear in reality gave his minions a way to zero in on you."

I crunched the ice cube and immediately regretted it. I had a sudden shooting pain in my head — ice cream headache. I let that fade, trying the trick of putting my tongue against the roof of my mouth. It never worked, but it was something to do until the excruciating pain went away.

Finally, when I could think again, I asked, "Why does Aeodymus want me? I know there's the whole 'event' thing. But why try to kidnap me? Why not just kill me? Not that I'm in a hurry or anything."

Xander smiled. "He has a plan, and you're part of it," he said. "Aeodymus is a particularly nasty *Teth*. The corrupt *Teth* have always played with reality, forcing it to take the shape of their will. But he's always taken it to extremes. All *Teth* can reshape reality, but most are cool about it. They tie their knots and create a story, and if they're skilled enough — and if the knotwork agrees to be a part of that story — reality will take the shape they want, and everything moves along nicely. So a *Teth* can turn a man into a frog without tearing a hole in reality, but only if the man's knotwork is ok with being a frog. Basically, if the man *wants* to be a frog, he'll be eating flies and sitting on lilypads in no time."

"Who would want to be a frog?" I asked.

Xander shrugged. "It happens. Sometimes subconsciously. There are people who turn into wolves every now and then. Some do it on purpose, while others change whenever there's a full moon, as if they had no control over it. Either they or some *Teth* wrote that into their story, manipulated their knotwork to make that a part of them. No tears in reality over things like that, unless that person didn't want to be a wolf. That happens, too."

I thought about this. "Is it the person's will, or does the knotwork itself have a will of its own?"

"Good question," Xander said, leaning back slightly and sipping mineral water from a straw. "The answer is yes."

"Yes?" I asked.

"The will of the person is part of the will of his or her knotwork, which is part of the will of the overall knotwork, throughout the Omni."

"So it's alive?" I asked.

"You tell me."

I looked around at everyone and everything in the cafe, on the street, along the sidewalks. The knotwork wove in and out of everything, in patterns that were infinitely complex. And everything was connected, in one way or another. Thin and wispy threads ran between everything. Thicker threads tied together families and friends. Everything had its bit of knotwork. Everything felt alive. "Yeah," I said then. "I think it is."

Xander had a small smile on his lips. He gave a quick nod, and said, "Not every *Teth* believes that. Some think that the knotwork is just a medium, like clay — there to be molded into what they want, whether it likes it or not. It's when a *Teth* forces the knotwork into a story it doesn't want that things get ugly. Threads get torn. Holes open in the fabric of the Omni. Things leak from one Layer to another."

"And that's what Aeodymus does?" I asked.

"Better than anyone else in the history of the Layers. He wants to reshape the Omni itself, to fit the story he has in mind. He started by conquering a few realities here and there. He had a nice cluster — a multiverse of his very own, in a sense. I discovered it, mostly because 8-Ball gave me clues. And I took some trusted *Teth* to confront him, and to undo the damage he caused."

"You built a snare, and trapped him on one of the Layers," I said, remembering. "Why not just kill him?"

Xander looked at me, sharply. "Would you?" he asked.

I blinked, but thought about it. "I don't know. Maybe? If all of reality was at stake, maybe I would."

Xander shook his head. "It's never as easy as that. It's never that cut and dry. There are men who understand killing, Sawyer. They're strong men, with strong wills. But they're torn inside. Their own knotwork has its kinks and loose threads, all of their own making. When you take a life, you remove a pattern from the fabric of reality. You're changing reality with that choice. You can argue that it's a just thing to do, and you may be right. I'm not a *Teth*, I can't see the knotwork or know the patterns or stories of reality. But I know that killing isn't something you should do, if you have any other choice. Aeodymus is dangerous. And maybe I regret my choice to imprison him, rather than kill him. But I've seen too much history, and too many mistakes start with killing someone because there seemed to be no other way to stop them."

I thought about this. "I guess I understand that," I said. "But I think, sometimes, you just have to change the story."

"Careful with that thinking," Xander warned. "That's how most wizards and gods get their start."

That shut me up. I hadn't met any wizards or gods yet, but I'd seen some of their handiwork. The last thing I wanted was to be the kind of person who would twist another human being, or reality itself, into something unnatural, just because I wanted to.

"But again, why me?" I asked, trying to move on, to get my head out of the mental landscape that featured me as an evil villain.

"You're not like other *Teth*," Xander said, staring into his glass of mineral water. "Most *Teth* have to actually create a pattern in order to manipulate the knotwork. They tie knots into string, or draw a knotwork pattern on a piece of paper, or engrave it into a piece of material. There's a mental component to what they do, it's true. But they need the physical pattern to shape the story. They energize it, let it connect to the knotwork and do the work it was meant to do. What you do, though, goes beyond that. You're able to not only perceive the knotwork, but change it with just your mind. That's profound. And that's why Aeodymus wants you, I think. He knows, somehow, what you can do. And he intends to force you to free him from his Layer, for a start. After that, I think he intends to use your power to shred the Omni and start over."

I listened to every word, but found myself lost in my own rabbit trail of thoughts from time to time. It was a little unnerving, to think that some apparently immortal and all-powerful god was trying to get his hands on me. "How can he force me to do what he wants? Can he control my mind?"

Xander shrugged. "Maybe. Some *Teth* have been able to do that. But it's more likely he'll try to use some sort of leverage to get you to do what he wants, willingly."

"What kind of leverage?" I asked.

Xander regarded me for a moment, silent. He took a swallow of his mineral water. Finally he said, "He has a way. Nothing you need to worry about."

"I'm pretty worried about it actually. What does he have that could force me to do what he wants? Maybe there's a way to protect myself from it."

Xander was silent and unmoving, continuing to stare into his drink. It was clear he was debating something.

Suddenly, out of seemingly nowhere, 8-Ball glided up to us. Xander looked around quickly, then grabbed him out of mid-air and put him in the chair in between us, where our bags here wedged between the chair back and the table. 8-Ball was silent, as always, but I got the impression that he didn't really like being grabbed.

"What do you want to do, get us on TV? This is one of the *boring* Layers, 8-Ball! They're just itching to see something unusual!"

8-Ball rose again, but this time stayed close to the surface of the table. It shook itself, and presented its message window to Xander.

"Outlook not so good," Xander read aloud. "Great."

"What does that mean?" I asked.

"It means we weren't able to shake them. There are probably some Inks on the way. This Layer doesn't have any tears, but the Inks can move from Layer to Layer without one. They're weaker than Quills and other Aeodymus minions, but no less dangerous."

"I've met a couple," I said.

"So I've heard. Untied one, from what your Gram said."

I looked down at the table top. Given Xander's position on killing, he might not be that pleased with me.

"Sawyer, don't worry. The Inks and Quills aren't alive, as such. It's a sort of life. But they were created by Aeodymus out of material from the In-Between. It's not like the rest of the Omni. It's dark stuff, and usually not all that friendly. What you untied wasn't a living creature, but a sort of artificial life. Still, I'd prefer if we didn't kill any more of them. I'm still hopeful we can find a way to make peace with them."

"Got it," I said. Though I secretly vowed that I'd untie an Ink or a Quill before I'd let either take me or harm someone I cared about. Xander had his principles, and I respected them. But I didn't share them. Not entirely. Not on this.

8-Ball nudged Xander, then shook itself and presented its message window again.

"Signs point to yes," Xander read. "Ok, let's get out of here."

"You're going to have to teach me your code some day," I asked.

"I've had thousands of years to work out a system with 8-Ball. Don't expect it to happen overnight."

I nodded. "Where to now? Or should I even bother asking? It's not like I'll recognize the place."

"You'll recognize this one. We're going back to the Long Land."

Before I could say anything, he snapped a button loose and opened the portal. All three of us went through, and Xander closed it behind us.

We exited on a long road that wound its way ahead and behind for obscure miles through trees and high grass. Once again I was taken by how *beautiful* the place was. How *perfect* in every way. Everything I could see was a perfect version of itself. It was sort of surreal and disorienting.

I was starting to realize that the world I knew — the world I grew up in — was a complex weave of imperfections. Without these imperfections things didn't feel *real*. The imperfections were what created *reality* for me.

"Isn't this the one place I'm supposed to avoid? I mean, other than Earth Prime?"

Xander laughed. "I can't believe he still calls it that."

"But this is where all the snares and Ticks and everything else are, right?"

"Yes. They're all over the Omni, really. Even Aeodymus doesn't have the ability to create an infinite army, however. Since there's no way to predict which Layers are infiltrated, it's safest to assume they're everywhere. And now, apparently, they've found a way to track my button holes. Which annoys me."

"How do you think they're doing it?" I asked.

Xander shook his head. Then stopped short, causing me to do the same. He turned to 8-Ball.

"Are they tracking me?" he asked.

8-Ball shook, and presented his answer.

"My reply is no," it said.

"Are they tracking Sawyer?"

Again 8-Ball shook. "Reply hazy, try again."

Xander groaned and rolled his eyes. "You cursed little thing, are you just here to torture me?"

8-Ball started to shake, but Xander reached out and grabbed him. "It was a rhetorical question!" he said. "And you know that!"

"Are they tracking something I'm carrying?" I asked.

Xander looked at me as 8-Ball shook. When the answer floated into the window, it read, "Yes."

Xander blinked. "Yes? In thousands of years, you have never answered 'yes' to anything. That's quite possibly the most direct answer you have ever given!"

8-Ball shook, and in the window a new message appeared. "Concentrate and ask again."

Xander and I looked at each other. "I'm pretty sure he means you," Xander said.

I thought for a moment. What could I be wearing that might be tracked by these things? If I started naming things at random we might be here just long enough for an Ink to find us. Better to narrow it down.

"Is it a piece of clothing?" I asked.

8-Ball answered, "My reply is no."

Ok, that narrowed it down a bit. "Is it in my bag?" I asked.

"My reply is no."

That made it a significantly small list. "Is it my pocket knife?"

"My reply is no."

That only left one thing, and it filled me with dread. "Is it the necklace?"

8-Ball shook, and I held my breath. The answer floated into view.

"Reply hazy, try again."

Xander and I exchanged looks. "What does that mean?" I asked.

Xander shook his head. "I'm not certain, but I think it means the necklace is part of the story, not all of it. Try to narrow it down further."

I thought about this for a moment, then asked, "Is it the braid?"

8-Ball shook, and I waited in dread until the answer appeared. "My reply is no."

I let out a breath. The braid was my only connection to Gram and Gramps, and the only means I had of "training" myself in all of this. Losing it would have been rough.

Still, something about the necklace was giving these things a way to track us.

"Is it the pattern?" I asked.

8-Ball shook, and the answer appeared. "Yes."

I looked at Xander. "I'm not sure how that can be. Gram made this necklace. It's supposed to help *prevent* detection."

"Maybe you should take it off and examine it," Xander said.

I nodded, and reluctantly pulled it up and over my head. Oddly, with it off, the whole world came into even more focus. I realized, then, that there was still a remnant of the old pattern — the one Gram had used to keep me from discovering what I could do too early. Apparently it hadn't been completely removed, only changed slightly when I ...

I smacked my forehead with the palm of my hand.

"Are you regretting that you didn't have a V8?" Xander asked.

I shook my head. "I don't even know what that means," I said. "But no. I'm regretting that I'm a forgetful idiot."

"What happened?"

I held up the necklace. "I altered this. It was the first thing I did, when I discovered the knotwork. I untied and retied Gram's pattern. And when I did, I must have somehow messed things up. It was still sort of half blocking my perception, for starters."

"What does the pattern say now?" Xander asked.

I spread the necklace on the ground, breaking contact with it completely, and stood back to get a better look at the knotwork. I recognized the patterns immediately. I'd seen them all my life, without quite knowing that I was seeing them. The stories were familiar — safety, hiding, and something that could only be described as "do not notice." There was also the braid, which was a hugely complex weave that told stories I couldn't grasp all at once. I wanted to follow those, to go deeper and learn more about my bloodline, about my abilities, about the Omni. I shook this off. Time for that later. I hoped.

Below the familiar patterns and the braid was something else, buried in the weave. It was so tiny, it blended almost perfectly into the overall pattern. Its story was one of tracking and detection. It was small, though. I could see it wouldn't have much range. Except …

"I found it," I said. "It's a sort of short-range tracker. And it seems to be tuned to the same sort of black knotwork that was wound through the Quill. Sort of black and gooey."

Xander was peering over my shoulder, though I knew he couldn't see what I was seeing. "The In-Between," he said quietly. "That's how they're tracking us."

"I don't get it," I said.

We straightened up, and Xander said, "When the *Teth* move between Layers, they open up the weave in the fabric of reality and more or less squeeze through. It's direct. You're really sort of riding the knotwork from one location to another. But when I move us from one reality to another, I essentially unbutton reality, opening a hole and then passing through. For a split instant we are actually in neither world, but in the In-Between. That is the realm that Aeodymus has more or less claimed as his own. He used the knotwork of that place to create his minions. I move through it freely. Nothing can get to me as I travel. Or never has, at any rate. But apparently we can be tracked by a tiny little short-range tracker. Every time we went through a button hole, they knew where we were. They were waiting for us to get near a tear, so they could make an attempt on you."

"But we shut that down. Can they still get to us?"

"They have your scent now, as it were," Xander said. "Once they had a point of reference, they could track where we went next. Again and again. It's only a matter of time before they manage to find a tear close enough to allow a crossover, and they'll be on their way."

I looked again at the necklace. "My fault. Again," I said.

Xander shook his head. "You had no idea. How could you? But we need to fix this, to remove the tracker. Now that they're on to us, I have to accelerate the time table on something."

"What? What time table? What's happening?"

Again Xander shook his head. "I'll explain, I promise. But for now, we need to destroy that necklace."

"No!" I said.

"I don't see that we have a choice, Sawyer. I know your Gram gave it to you ..."

"It's more than that! It links me back to her, but it has the braid woven into it. That's one of the oldest things in creation, Gram said."

"She says things like that a lot. It may not be true," Xander replied. There was the hint of a quirky smile on his face, and for the first time I found I wanted to smack him.

"I'm not destroying it," I said.

"Well we can't keep carrying it with us," he replied.

He was right. We couldn't just ignore it. The tracker would eventually lead them right to us. We'd have to run, again and again, just because I couldn't let go of this necklace made of twine and string.

I looked at it, through the knotwork. I had learned a lot since the first time I untied and retied this. I could see the tracker now. Maybe I could fix it.

"Don't," Xander said.

I ignored him, and reached into the knotwork with my mind, following the threads of it as they wove into the necklace. When I came to the tracker, it was like smacking into a wall at high speed. The little thing was protected, and it was a far more complex protection than anything I'd seen so far.

Also, the size of the tracker was deceptive. It was small, but it was complex. Far more complex than I had suspected. How had it gotten there? It must have been carried by a Tick, and may have been placed into the knotwork years earlier. Gram had clearly never noticed it was there. It must have been waiting for the day when she would inevitably bring me to Xander, who would move us through the In-Between.

Aeodymus could play a long game.

The small knot of dark thread was tight, nearly impossible to work with. And it was ... well, the only word I could think of was "gross." It was something from outside of reality, and inherently disgusting to me. But in function, it was the same as any knotwork. It had a pattern and a story. It could be manipulated.

Slowly, painfully, I managed to work my way into it. This, I knew, was dangerous — like what I'd done with Edgar. My own knotwork was invested in this now. And even though the tracker was microscopic, the size didn't seem to matter as much as the complexity. I was committed now, tied to this thing from outside of reality, and the only way I could be free of it was to untie it.

I started to work the knot, to try to create slack so I could begin untying it. This seemed to work, at first. But I quickly found that the slack I created in one part only tightened another. The knotwork was so well designed that trying to unravel it just made it stronger.

Too late I realized what this meant.

I tried to pull free of the knotwork, to snap back to reality, but I couldn't. The more I pulled, the tighter the grip. I struggled, tried to force my way out, but couldn't break free.

I was stuck.

As I looked frantically for a way out, I kept running into roadblocks. A twist I thought might be easy to unravel suddenly became a tar pit of smaller knots and loops, sucking me deeper into it. At a point, I stopped struggling altogether, and instead felt an overwhelming despair. It was hopeless. I was trapped, and would be forever. I would never see the outside world again. I would never see Gram or Gramps or Xander.

This was it then. The end of Sawyer Jackson. It was a short book, and maybe not all that interesting to read. But I knew, with no doubt whatsoever, that my life was completely over. I would spend the rest of eternity trapped in a tiny knotwork made of darkness.

❁❈❃❉❊❋❉❃❈❁

I wasn't sure how long I'd been there. My best estimate was around ten thousand years. Maybe more. Maybe less. Honestly, time had no meaning whatsoever in that place. My thoughts would race one instant, and drag like molasses the next. In one swipe I would see the entire sixteen years of my life and memories play out like one long movie, and then all those moments would shatter, replaced by alternate stories that belonged in horror movies.

I had nightmares of Gram and Gramps beating me mercilessly, forcing me to be their slave. I screamed as Xander Travel tore me apart with his bare hands, consuming me a bite at a time. I lived a thousand nightmares of being tortured, my life being drawn into one long spiral of pain and fear and despair.

You're an interesting one, a voice said, after eons of this suffering.

"Who's there?" I shouted. "Who is that?" I was afraid. More afraid than I'd ever been in my life.

You were foolish again. I blame your youth. You had your experience with Edgar, but learned nothing. How disappointing.

I didn't recognize the voice. It wasn't Xander. It wasn't anyone I knew. It was just there, in my mind. I could *feel* it.

You will do very nicely.

"Do what?" I asked. The dread and fear were back, stronger than ever.

You will free me. And when you do, I will weave the Omni into a new story. The story of me. A new and glorious age will begin. And you will make all of it possible.

I knew, then. There was no doubt. "Aeodymus," I said.

I am so pleased you've heard of me, young Sawyer Jackson. I know absolutely everything about you, now that you've entangled yourself in one of my creations.

"The tracker," I said. Saying it reminded me, renewed my will, and again I struggled, trying to find a way to untie the knot, to free myself.

There was a chuckle, dark and low, in my mind.

You can never escape, Sawyer. This knot cannot be untied. None of my knotwork can be undone.

"I untied an Ink," I said.

True. I've seen that. Most impressive. But you were a bit more hands on in that process, I believe. You didn't so much unite the knotwork as tear through it, isn't that true?

He was right. I had used my pocket knife to slice into the thing, to cut out the knotwork that made it "alive." That wasn't quite the same as untying it. I despaired again. It was hopeless.

Good. That is the obedience I seek. You will make a nice pet, Sawyer Jackson. Your ability is profound. You have no idea. It very nearly matches my own.

"What are you going to do to me?" I asked

I'm going to devour you. I'm going to untie you, and weave you into myself. Through you, I will walk among the Layers again. I will untie those as well, and tie them into myself, and grow. You, Sawyer Jackson, are what I have waited for through all my existence. The event you were created for was this. You will be my instrument, and I will use you to destroy all that is, and remake it as it should be.

"I'll never help you," I said.

He laughed.

No, I suspect you will not. There is no need. Your will has nothing to do with how you will be used. I will leave you intact, however. It will be a great amusement to me, to see you suffer as I use your own power to unmake the Omni. Yours will be the only story I leave from the old world. A great honor. Everything else — your Gram, your Gramps, that accursed Xander Travel, even that annoying Akashic Sphere — all will be shredded, tied into whatever lowly bit of feces or filth I deem to allow existence. All will suffer, Sawyer Jackson. All those who opposed me and trapped me here. All will be made into the lowliest of creation, and left to rot. And I will laugh, if ever I bother to remember them.

The despair became overwhelming. Far from struggling now, all I wanted was oblivion. All I wanted was to *not exist* anymore. I stared into the darkness, unable to see any trace of the knotwork, or of life. The infinite blackness flowed over me, enclosing me. All was dark and hopeless and infinitely black.

Except ...

A small dot in the distance. The rest of the universe was utter blackness, but there in the distance was a tiny pinprick of light. I moved toward it.

No, no, Sawyer Jackson. That is not for you. Turn away, or be destroyed.

I ignored him. His voice spiraled through me, but was not a part of me. He was surrounding me, digging into every corner of my mind, uncovering everything that made me who I was. But he couldn't change it. That was what I realized, as I got closer to the light. Aeodymus could see everything I was, but in order to use me I would have to give him control. I almost had. I had come so very close. But now there was a small pinprick of hope.

The light became a thread. And the thread became a pattern. I followed this.

Do not go any further, Sawyer Jackson, or I will untie you.

I kept moving. Destroying me, here and now, wouldn't serve his purpose. I wasn't convinced he could even do it. As I moved along the pattern, I became less and less convinced of it. I could feel his power over me slipping. I could feel my mind clearing. I could see more than before. I could understand more of what was happening to me.

And then I came to the wall.

It wasn't actually a wall, but a tight weave of dark knotwork.

No further, Aeodymus said, and I heard a sound of amusement in his voice. Or rather, I *felt* his amusement. He had let me get this far, to experience hope, so that he could crush it.

He still had me trapped, and I could sense a dark chuckle as he saw me realize it.

And then I heard a different voice.

"Sawyer, my sweet boy."

I recognized it immediately. "Gram?" I whispered. It sounded like her, but different.

"You've gotten yourself into a bit of trouble, I see."

"I'm trapped! I can't get out!"

"Don't panic. Stay calm. Do you see the pattern? The light?"

"Yes!"

Begone, woman! The boy is mine!

"I can hear the buzzing of that useless old creature," she said.

That made me smile. And when I did, the light brightened.

"I see it!" I said. "What do I do?"

"That is the braid, Sawyer. That is the history of our entire bloodline. Older than Aeodymus. Stronger. Follow it."

I followed. But it wasn't easy. The black knotwork clung to me, wrapped itself around me and refused to loosen. Every bit of progress I made was a struggle, like pulling myself free from a tar pit.

"You're as far in as you can go," she said. "Now you will have to untie the black knotwork."

"But I can't!" I cried. "I tried, and failed."

"You have to," she said. "I can't help you with this part, Sawyer. You have to do it yourself. You're tangled in it, and you're the only one who can get you untangled. You have to try!"

I looked back into the inky darkness and cringed.

You will never be free, Sawyer. I own you. This is your world now. Blackness. Emptiness. Loneliness. You will never leave this place.

I felt a tug from the black knotwork, and part of me wanted to let go, to let it just drag me back in and engulf me forever.

I dug in, grasped the braid, and started into the dark knotwork, suddenly filled with rage. I saw, all at once, that the despair, the loss of hope, was coming from this black goo of a pattern. And I saw that if I couldn't pull myself free, this would be the fate of everything in the Omni. Aeodymus would somehow use my abilities to destroy all that was, and replace it with this repugnant mass.

I wasn't going to let that happen.

I reached out. I had a firm grip on the braid, the *real* knotwork, and I reached out into the twist of wormlike threads that spiraled into the darkness. I found one that was tied to me, and worked at it for a moment, pulling it loose. It tightened elsewhere, but I was ready for that. I reached out with my mind and held both parts of the knot, and worked them together until I created the opening I was looking for.

That was all it took. I didn't have to solve the entire pattern, just this one piece. Pulling it free, loosening the threads, I saw the dark knotwork start to open and unravel. In a moment, I could see light pouring through in irregular patches. And a moment beyond that, it all fell to pieces.

I gasped and sat up. I was covered in sweat, and dressed in night clothes. I was in a large bed, in a room I didn't recognize.

Gram was sitting next to me, her head resting on the edge of the bed, grasping my hand in hers. She looked up, startled, and smiled. She looked as tired I felt.

"You're back!" she said, and kissed the back of my hand. Tears were streaming down her face.

I tried to speak, but choked. She quickly reached out and grabbed a glass of water from the nightstand, giving it to me but holding it as I drank. "Slowly," she said. "Not too fast. You've been tangled for the past three days. You're dehydrated."

"Three days?" I rasped.

"Xander brought you here, to the cabin, and called for us to return. It's risky here, but it's the safest place in the Long Land, at the moment. We were very worried about you, sweetie. What you did was *very* dangerous."

I nodded. "I know. I'm sorry."

She looked at me, smiling a tired little smile. "But look at you! I was so worried. I hoped and prayed you'd find your way out, and you did!"

"You got me out," I said, then coughed a little before sipping more water. "Thank you."

She looked at me with a strange expression. "What did I have to do with it?" she asked.

"You came to me, and showed me the way out," I said.

She look her head, smiling. "No, Sawyer. I didn't. I couldn't reach you. I tried, again and again, but you were too mired in that black knotwork. I couldn't find a way to reach you. I must have knitted a blanket big enough for an elephant, and still I couldn't manage it! I was almost convinced you were gone for good."

I thought about this, confused. "But I *heard* you," I said. "I heard your voice, telling me how to get out."

She regarded me for a moment, and asked, "You heard a voice that sounded like mine?"

I nodded.

She laughed, a small laugh that had just a note of sadness to it. "Well, isn't that sweet — she's still alive after all. After all this time. And she's still looking after you."

"Who?" I asked.

She gave my hand a squeeze, and with a tear rolling down her cheek, she said, "Your mother, Sawyer. That was your mother's voice. She's the one who saved you."

NINE | PLANS CHANGE

It was difficult to sit up, but I managed. Gramps brought a tray into the room that was absolutely piled with food. And every bit of it was perfect and delicious. There is something pretty sweet about eating "ultimate bacon" — the bacon upon which all *other* bacon is based — and washing it down with "ultimate coffee." A boy could get used to it.

For all the ultimate deliciousness, though, I didn't have much of an appetite. Too much had happened, and too many questions had come to the surface.

Xander, with 8-Ball hovering nearby, sat in a big, plush chair next to my bed. Gram sat on a corner of the bed itself. She hadn't left me alone since I'd woken up.

"So, that won't happen again, right?" Xander asked. "Because that seems to keep happening with you."

"No," I said. "God, I hope not." The queasiness increased a bit.

"Except when we need it to," Xander said.

Gram gave him a hard look. "Which had better be *never*," she said.

Xander shook his head. "He's got a lot of talent, Liv. You should have trained him."

"I trained him *plenty*," Gram said. "How do you think he knows all this stuff?"

"You trained me?" I asked. "Was I there for that?"

She smiled, then thumped my forehead, hard. "Don't sass mouth me," she said. "Of *course* I trained you. Just because you didn't recognize it at the time doesn't mean I let things slide."

"Think *Karate Kid*," Gramps said. "Wax on, wax off. Tie knot. Untie knot."

"I didn't do a lot of knot tying when I was a kid," I said, frowning.

"More than you think. You're having trouble remembering because I went to great pains to keep your from *noticing* the knotwork. I was constantly having to take string away from you, when you were a baby. Later, you would doodle with crayons or something and I'd have to get you to go play outside or whatever, before you could accidentally energize a pattern."

"So this whole time, I was learning, but didn't know I was learning," I said. The idea of this bothered me for some reason.

"Yes, mostly. And I'm sorry, sweetie, it's just the way it had to be. With so many monstrous things looking for you, I wasn't sure how safe you'd be. There were a couple of close calls, when you were younger. I had to hide the whole house more than once. So your Gramps and I decided it was best if we kept you from getting too involved with the knotwork. It was better this way."

I wasn't sure how true that was. What was better about it? Keeping me safe — was that justification enough to lie to me for sixteen years? Maybe it was. If I trusted Gram and Gramps, I would also have to trust their decisions. Wouldn't I?

"Ok, fine," I said. "But now I know, and now I'm in *real* danger, because I don't know everything I *should*."

She looked at me for a long moment — long enough that that little part of me that wants to be a good boy, and wants never to make her angry, was starting to get antsy. Then she said, "You're right. I had hoped to keep you from this life for as long as possible. I was wrong, about a lot of things."

Again tears were rolling down her cheek, and I immediately lost the resolve to be angry with her.

"It's done," Xander said. "Undoing it would get messy."

I started to ask how you could "undo" something like that, but he raised a hand and cut me off.

"Time is just like anything else in the Omni. If you're willing to screw everything up, there are ways to do that. It's one of the dangers posed by Aeodymus. Time and space are what we're protecting. But my point is that your past brought you to where you are now, and made you who you are at the same time. This is where we need you, Sawyer. And you are who we need."

"No pressure or anything," I said.

"All the pressure that ever existed, actually. But no, beyond that, no pressure."

"So I take it my showdown with Aeodymus wasn't the 'event' I was born for?"

Xander laughed. "You thought it was?"

I shook my head. "No, not really. He tried to convince me that it was, but I think I knew, even then. It's just … that was *hard*, Xander. The hardest thing I've ever done, and I nearly blew it. I was ready to give up until …"

"Until your mother came to help," Gram said, smiling, her eyes glistening. Crying wasn't something Gram did often, but when she started anything could trigger it.

"About that," Xander said, turning to Gram. "How could she do that, given the circumstances?"

"What circumstances?" I asked.

Gram ignored me. "Our bloodline is connected to the braid. It's a sort of family heirloom. So in some sense, everyone in our bloodline is connected to it, if even by the thinnest thread, right up until we die."

Xander nodded. "Which means she's still alive. All of them may be," he said.

"All of who?" I asked. Then, suddenly, I got angry. "Listen, I've had *enough* of people keeping secrets from me. It hasn't worked out well so far." I looked around the room, and for once everyone looked sheepish, avoiding eye contact with me. "What *happened?* How does it involve my mother?"

"It involved both your parents, actually," Xander said. "And a number of other *Teth*. All of them gave their lives to create the snare that holds Aeodymus in his prison Layer. At least, that's what we've always believed."

I blinked, and felt tears of my own finally start. I hadn't thought much about my mother, over the years. I had no memory of her or my father. My whole life, the only mother and father I knew were my Gram and Gramps. They told me stories of my parents, and told me they "had to go away," which I eventually determined to mean they were dead. I never asked how, though I wasn't sure why. Maybe Gram worked a knotwork around the question. Maybe I wasn't *allowed* to ask. I bit back a bitterness that was rising within me, and reminded myself that with the whole of reality at stake, and the outcome possibly riding on my shoulders, a few secrets was a small price to pay for even the hint of a normal childhood. Gram and Gramps had given me a gift, I decided.

I didn't quite believe it yet, but with time I hoped I would.

"She's still alive," I said. "And she's trapped there."

Xander nodded. "So it seems. And Sawyer, you have to remember, her life — the lives of all those *Teth* — that wasn't the only cost. To hold Aeodymus, we had to sacrifice an entire *Layer*. That's a *universe*, mired in a snare, and overrun by a very powerful man bent on destroying and reshaping reality. Earth is only one world in that universe. There are millions of inhabited worlds, with life of every description. When we trapped Aeodymus there, we sacrificed all of those lives. A universe of life, to hold one man. I tell you this so you have some perspective on just how dangerous Aeodymus is."

"I have some idea," I said, remembering my battle to free myself from the muck and mire of his dark knotwork.

Xander shook his head. "I'm sorry, but you don't. What you experienced is nothing. It's mild. You're going to face much worse. So we're going to need you to learn as much as you can, as fast as you can."

"He has the braid," Gram said. "It's been feeding him information ever since he started carrying it."

"Too passive," Xander said. "It'll take too long."

"I can do searches," I said. Everyone looked at me, confused. "Like Google." If it was possible, everyone managed to look even *more* confused. I rolled my eyes. "I found a way to go into the braid and ask questions, to search for information I need."

"How?" Gram asked, her face lighting with pride.

I shook my head. "It's kind of hard to explain. But basically I imagine the shape of what I want to know, and if anything matches that shape or even just comes close to it, the idea and the reality sort of connect, like two magnets. The braid fills in missing details in what I'm imagining. Does that make sense?"

They all stared at me. Xander and Gram exchanged looks. "Does it?" Xander asked.

"I've never heard of anyone doing that before. I mean, you can concentrate on the braid and let your mind wander, and it fills you in on our family history and that sort of thing. That's how it has always been used. But this … I've never heard of a *Teth* being able to do something like this."

"He's able to manipulate the knotwork without creating a physical pattern," Xander said. "I've seen him do it."

She nodded. "We have too. Well, mostly. He used to make patterns in the air, with his hands."

"I'm right here, you know." I was feeling a little irritated. A lot seemed to happen *to* me or *around* me, but precious little seemed to happen *with* me.

"Don't get snippy," Gram said. "We have as much to adjust to in this as you do. It's one new discovery after another with you."

"And that's saying a lot," Xander said. "I've been around for a very long time, and it's not every day I meet someone who can do things I've never seen before."

"What can I say?" I held up my hands in what I thought of as a "grand" pose, "I am the great and all-powerful wizard!"

Gram gasped and, to my shock, slapped me.

I was so stunned I forgot to put my arms down. Instead, I just looked at her, wide-eyed. It hadn't hurt, the slap. Not much. It was a slight sting that lingered long after she'd recoiled and covered her mouth with the hand that had just struck me. In all my life she'd never laid a hand on me like that.

"I'm … Sawyer I'm so sorry! It's just …"

"Don't call yourself a wizard, son," Gramps said. "The name has some pretty heavy baggage among the *Teth*."

I lowered my arms, and touched my cheek, which felt warm and still stung a little. "I see," I said. I felt a cold sensation come over me, like dread. *Anger*. All the pieces were snapping together — the lies and the manipulations, hiding the truth of who I was and who my parents were — and I didn't like how those pieces fit. It would be too easy to mold myself into the shape of them.

"Don't be angry with her," Xander said. "Tensions are high. It was a reaction, and she regrets it."

"I do," she whispered. She was crying again, looking at me, not making an effort to touch me, which was good. "I do, Sawyer. I'm so sorry."

I took a deep breath and let it out slowly, calming myself. I couldn't quite let it go, not yet. But it would pass, I thought. Instead of keeping it at the center of conversation, I looked at Xander and said, "The timetable. Before I got into trouble with Aeodymus, you mentioned that the time table would have to be accelerated. Which means there's a plan I don't know about. What is it?"

Xander shook his head. "It's nothing."

"More nothing?" I asked. I couldn't keep the bitterness out of my voice.

He looked at me, then nodded. "Ok, then. Even your grandparents don't know about this. But maybe it's time everyone did." He looked at 8-Ball, who suddenly hovered up next to him. "Or is it?" he asked.

8-Ball shook, and Xander read the answer. "Yes."

He laughed. "That's only the second time I've gotten a straight answer out of him. It's a miracle."

"What's the plan?" Gramps asked. "What sort of trouble have you been plotting?"

Xander looked at him for a moment. "It's not going to be easy. Or fun. But I may have a way to counter Aeodymus, to negate his abilities once and for all."

"And kill him?" Gram asked.

Xander looked at her, sad. "If we must."

"Xander, I admire your commitment to preserving life," Gramps said. "But this is an evil so big, I can't believe that even you would let it continue."

"I'm in no position to judge which life is worth saving and which is worth ending," Xander said. "One day, we'll all be in the White Room. But for now, we have another, darker destination."

"Where?" Gram asked.

He hesitated, then said. "The Shadow Strait."

Gram inhaled sharply. "You're joking!"

"Almost always. But not this time."

I was confused. "What's the Shadow Strait?" I asked.

"It's a hole in the Omni!" Gram said, outraged. "And it's forbidden!"

Xander scoffed. "Forbidden, true. But only because it scares people."

"Forbidden because no one who has entered the Strait has *ever come back*," Gram said.

Xander smiled. "Almost no one."

Gram looked from him to Gramps, who shrugged. She turned back. "You've been there?"

"Once, yes."

"Xander … what would possess you? Why would you think that even you could survive in the Shadow Strait?"

"It was a dark time for me. Literally and figuratively. Entering into oblivion sounded appealing at the time." He raised a hand. "Don't ask. It's not something I like to talk about. But at any rate, I realized two things in my experience there. The first was that I wasn't really suited for oblivion. The second was that I was not the first to have gone in and returned."

"Who else?" Gramps asked.

"Aeodymus," Xander said. "When I was there, I met several creatures. They were drawn to me, to the light of my knotwork, I think. And they kept saying the name, over and over. They thought I was him. When they found I wasn't, I knew it was time to leave."

"I don't even know how to think about this," Gram said. "It's supposed to be impossible. I've known people who fell in, usually trying to skirt the Strait in boats, to shortcut to the other side. They never came back."

"It's true, going in is a lot easier than getting out," Xander said. "It took some effort, and some time. But I was less equipped for it than we will be."

"What could we possible carry with us that will get us out of the Shadow Strait?"

"More like 'who,'" Xander said, nodding at me.

Gram glanced at me quickly, then stood and started toward Xander. Gramps put a hand on her shoulder. She stopped, but I knew that it was a reflex. If she really wanted to get to Xander, Gramps wouldn't be able to stop her. No one would.

"He nearly *died* in your care, Xander Travel. I've trusted you with my life more than once, more than a thousand times. But I don't know that I can trust you with his!"

"You don't have to," Xander said. "You're going with me. So is Drew," he said, nodding to Gramps. "You're right. He's not safe with me, not alone. He needs training. More than he can get from the braid alone, I think."

Gramps stepped in beside Gram and said, "Why are we even going? What's in the Shadow Strait that's so important?"

"I believe it's where Aeodymus learned to tie the dark knotwork, for starters. But also, I think it's where he's hiding …" Xander glanced at me, stopping in mid-sentence.

"More secrets?" I asked. I had watched and listened to this conversation play out, happy enough to be an observer, to be on the inside of the plans for once. Now I felt that cold sensation grip me again. I felt the resentment growing. I pushed it back. Instead of resenting them, I would do what I could to get them to finally be honest and open with me. Anger and resentment wouldn't help with that.

It was a perfectly logical idea, and one I knew I should stick to. And yet, I could still feel that bitter cold, and that twist in my gut. This wasn't going to be easy.

Xander sighed. "No. No more secrets," he said. "One of the reasons we were forced to trap Aeodymus instead of, instead of killing him — one of the reasons was that we *couldn't* kill him — was that he wasn't really *there*."

"Wasn't there?" I asked. "What does that mean?"

Xander shook his head. "Hundreds of *Teth* stood against him, and all tried to take him down. Again and again he withstood anything they threw at him. And that was when we realized we weren't fighting Aeodymus at all. Not really."

"What were we fighting?" I asked quietly.

"Some sort of avatar. A simulacrum of Aeodymus. It was his will, and his power. It looked like him and thought like him. It spoke in his voice. It could manipulate the knotwork just as he had. But his *self* wasn't there. Some of the *Teth*, the more perceptive of them, noticed that there was a tendril of dark knotwork stretching off into infinity. It started within him, forming a pattern where the heart of his own knotwork should be. Whatever this thing was, it was being controlled by Aeodymus from somewhere far away. But it was not Aeodymus himself."

Gram shook her head. "I still don't believe that. If it wasn't him, why did the snare work?"

Xander shrugged. "I have theories, but no answers. At the moment, I believe the unique nature of the snare somehow trapped his consciousness in that form."

"Ok," I said. "I have questions boiling out of my brain right now, so I'm going to start with the most obvious first. Are you saying that somewhere in the Shadow Strait, we're going to find Aeodymus?"

Xander smiled. "I think so, yes. Though, if he's there, he's been inactive for a very long time. Those creatures thought I was him. Which means they haven't seen him in a while."

"Alright," I said. "And my next question — what was so special about the snare the *Teth* built to keep him on that Layer?"

Again Xander and Gram exchanged glances. I looked into their knotwork, and saw that despite everything they were preparing to lie to me. "I can see the lies forming tangles in both of you," I said.

"Sawyer! That's rude!" Gram said.

"Seriously?" I asked. "Knotwork etiquette? I'm trying really hard not to be bitter and angry here, after finding out that my whole life has been one big manipulation since a few thousand years before I was born. So please, just humor me and treat me like I'm actually human, and tell me the truth!"

Gram rushed to my side again, and before I could object or fight back she folded me into a hug, kissing my forehead, squeezing me tight. "I'm so sorry, sweetie. You're right. I'm sorry."

I could smell her perfume, and the scent of fabric softener she liked to use. I could feel the warmth of her hug. It was too much. I couldn't hold on to the anger, then. I had missed her while I was away with Xander. I was homesick. *She* was my home. I forgave her then, and finally the ice melted.

When she pulled away, I realized with embarrassment that I was crying. I wiped my eyes with the sleeve of my shirt. "Tell me about the snare," I said, looking for anything that would take the attention off of me.

"Ok," Xander said, nodding. "You're right. It's time." He took a seat in the plush chair again. Gramps sat on the other side of the bed. And we listened.

TEN | SNARES

Xander settled into the chair, and crossed his legs. He tented his fingers and closed his eyes, as if focusing all of his attention on the story.

"Aeodymus had torn through a number of Layers, establishing a foothold in several realities. And by foothold, I mostly mean he tore them to shreds. I spent a lot of time undoing the damage he'd done. And it wasn't easy. At the time, I had a team of *Teth* who helped me find and fix tears in the Layers. They were a great bunch of folks," He paused with this, inhaling and exhaling slowly. "I miss them." He tilted his head until his chin rested on his chest, shook his head slowly, then raised back up, as if looking through his closed eyelids.

"I was on his trail for quite some time, and it was irritating me. When one of the *Teth* came to me with word that they'd found him, I quickly gathered the best of my people, and we buttoned our way to that Layer, ready for anything. We thought.

"The place was a disaster. Foul creatures were leaking in through tears that stretched as wide as planets, in some cases. The Earth was barely recognizable. Other worlds were gone completely. The inhabitants of that universe were in various stages of torture, imprisonment — death, if they were lucky.

"The ruin that used to be an entire universe — it made me want to vomit. It was the most horrible scene I'd ever witnessed. And yet it was actually worse than I thought.

"We knew Aeodymus was insane, and bent on doing a lot of damage. But we never quite put the pieces together until that moment. He wasn't just randomly targeting universes, conquering and moving on to stay out of our reach. He was experimenting, trying to find a way to undo the whole thing. His goal was to wreck the Omni, and it was here, on this Layer, that he'd finally found a way to do it.

"Our arrival in that Layer had not gone unnoticed. Almost immediately multiple snares were triggered. Some came with traps that injured or even killed some of my people. But we didn't have time to mourn them. We were too busy defending ourselves from the monsters.

"I don't use that word lightly. These were more than just Inks or Quills. There was every variety of nightmare on that Layer, and they were pouring out of every wound in the universe. Hordes of them. They spread like cockroaches across everything, and they knew instantly that we had arrived.

"We fought, taking out as many as we could. Even I was forced to kill, in those days. I couldn't afford to hesitate, with so much at stake. My own personal views on life and death couldn't be a factor. At that moment, there on that Layer, facing the hordes of the enemy of all reality, I had to choose to fight rather than stick by my principles. I wish I could say I have no regrets about it, but it's not true. Even though those creatures were not life as we knew it, they were still alive — they still had potentials and futures. And I was ending that." Again he paused, the weight of the tale showing on his face, in the slump of his shoulders.

"But worse, there were lives lost that meant *more* to me than my principles. My brothers in that battle, the *Teth* who stood beside me for years of fighting — years of *losing* — were falling in front of me.

"And we *were* losing — there was no doubt about that. We would not win this fight, and we all knew it. As the enemy kept us engaged, Aeodymus continued to tear at the fabric of reality. We were able to prevent him from leaving and going to another Layer to start again while we remained on that world, fighting an endless war. The *Teth* figured that part out. And it cost them. Because the only way to prevent travel for Aeodymus was to prevent it for themselves. They bound their own knotwork into the fabric of that reality, creating one universal snare.

"Ironically, perhaps, it was Aeodymus who made this possible. He had shredded so much of the story of the universe, it made it easier for the *Teth* to gather in all the threads and weave them into their own. They became part of the Layer that day. Which is too much for any *Teth*. Even a shredded universe is vast. As each of them wove themselves into it, they vanished. Those of us who remained thought they were gone for good.

"We fought on for a time, but realized that losing there, on that battlefield, would be the end. Our sacrifice would serve no tactical advantage. It wouldn't stop Aeodymus, who would continue to look for a way to escape. Those *Teth* who had sacrificed themselves — they'd bought us time. They'd given us an advantage. We couldn't let their sacrifice be for nothing.

"I gathered the remaining *Teth*, many of whom insisted on staying and continuing the fight. I gave them no choice. I couldn't leave them behind. So I took them, even if it was against their will. My ability to travel among the Layers is different. Maybe a little less elegant. It's unhampered by things like the snare in the knotwork. In an instant, the *Teth* and I stepped from a roiling battle and into a peaceful Layer, in a different cluster.

"The *Teth* who had objected — most of them never forgave me for pulling them out of there. Some spent their lives trying to find a way back in, to rejoin the fight. They formed armies, taking the reprieve from battle as an opportunity to draw reinforcements.

"There are ways for *Teth* to extend their lives. It's similar to the way Exemplars — my people — managed to have a sort of immortality, though it's a bit more limited. Moving among the Layers has a side effect, of sorts. It effectively slows the clock. If you move around enough, you get the benefit of new hours. They cling to you, from universe to universe, adding to your overall reserve. And if you are a particularly talented *Teth*, you can manipulate your own knotwork to keep yourself strong and vital and even young. You can more or less choose the age you want to be, at least in appearance. The limitation is that the knotwork tends to resist when a *Teth* tries to change *others*. Changing someone's shape and appearance seems to be ok with the Omni, if that person's knotwork agrees. But prolonging their life — altering someone else's "life force," as it were — the Omni resists that. Blocks it, actually. There is clearly a purpose for death, even if we hate it.

"All that to say, some of the *Teth* who came back from that battle used their abilities to prolong their lives, to give them time to recruit armies. They wanted to go back. They couldn't live with just keeping Aeodymus trapped. They had to find a way to *destroy* him. Some even wanted to untie him altogether — to make his story unravel and leave him in threads to be swept away by the wind.

"I knew this would only lead to trouble. I am the last remaining Exemplar, and so I'm the only one with the ability to move between Layers without manipulating the knotwork. Or so I believed, for a very long time. Apparently there are some in the Omni with big, juicy brains, who can create machines that let them move from reality to reality. As it turns out, your Gramps was one of those.

"He's a smart man, though I hate admitting it. I don't even have to open my eyes to see his smug expression right now.

"Your Gramps created something that let him more or less 'button' his way across realities. Not quite the same, but similar enough. His very first trip carried him to the Long Land. He came at a turbulent time. Wizards were everywhere, abusing their ability to manipulate the knotwork. There was a sort of 'Cult of Aeodymus' that sprang up. They were fascinated by his ability to manipulate *entire universes*. They saw the allure of that — reshaping reality to suit you. There are infinite universes, so why not divvy them up among each *Teth*? Everyone can become a god in their own reality. The *Teth* should rule, they reasoned, because they had the power.

"Not all *Teth* felt this way, of course. Most didn't, in fact. The *Teth* have a sort of affinity for the Omni and the knotwork. They have a nearly physical reaction when things are twisted or tortured into the wrong shape. It's repugnant to them. So the thought of being like Aeodymus wasn't popular. Some *Teth* went to the extreme of denying their own abilities, and even punishing other *Teth*, if they suspected them of being wizards. It was the birth of a millennia of class loathing, which I sometimes question. I've met wizards who *aren't* bent on destroying the fabric of reality, who try to use their abilities for good, without quite recognizing the long-term consequences of tearing holes in the knotwork. They're misguided individuals, taking shortcuts to achieve their goals. Some of them suffered horribly for it.

"At any rate, when your grandfather arrived here in the Long Land, the very nature of his technology made the *Teth* think he *had* to be a wizard. He got on the bad side of many *Teth*, who wanted to imprison him, or worse.

"One of those *Teth* was your Gram. I won't go into their story — that's theirs to tell. But let's just say, there is rarely a scenario where two people end up getting married and having children after one of them actively tries to murder the other.

"While all that drama and eventual romance was happening, however, I recognized another problem altogether. The machine your Gramps built was incredibly dangerous. It was a tempting target for both sides of the war. The Wizards wanted it, because it would allow them to move among the Layers without worrying about snares. Those who were truly fanatical about Aeodymus could even use it to free him.

"Equally dangerous, however, were the remaining *Teth* who were building armies to face off with Aeodymus again. Those *Teth* who served with me in battle — they had not forgotten. Many of them were still alive, and still vital. They had extended their lives, constantly moving among the Layers, continuously manipulating their own knotwork. They planned to be ready for the day when they could go back. And when word of your grandfather reached them, they came in force. They wanted that technology.

"I couldn't let that happen. In the time since that battle, I'd had the chance to learn a few things of my own. The *Teth* who remained loyal to me had shared all they knew about Aeodymus, and the strange dark thread that connected him to this avatar we faced in the torn Layer. Using that information, I was eventually able to determine that Aeodymus was hiding out somewhere in the Omni, with his knotwork linked to the avatar by that thread. I thought for a time that he was in the In-Between. That seemed to be where all of his creations came from. They clearly live and breed there, with each generation firmly tied to his will. But after my experience in the Shadow Strait, I'm now convinced he's in there, hidden so well that even his own minions can't find him.

"I believe the creatures I met there are actually natural-born. I think they're a sort of dark-thread version of life here, in the Omni. The strait could lead to a super reality outside of the Omni — a sort of *Dark* Omni. No one likes this theory. But if you think about it, we know that universes seem to have an affinity for replication. There are clusters of alternate realities — multiverses that are independent of each other. Those multiverses are clustered into the Omni, like grapes in a bowl. Why couldn't there be *another* Omni out there?" He sighed. "It's a very unpopular theory. But I think it has merit."

He finally opened his eyes. "There's more, of course. I could sit here and talk for an eternity, but those are the facts that matter most."

He looked at each of us, then shook his head.

"Except one," he said. "There's one story you need to know. It's a short story, which makes it sad. But years after your Gramps arrived in the Long Land, after all the drama was sorted and your Gram was no long trying to kill him, they were a nice, happy family. Your Gram made some tough choices around that time. One of them was to limit her movement on the Layers. She chose to grow old with your Gramps. It's a noble choice, and one I respect. But her daughter — your mother — wanted to explore the Omni as other *Teth* could do. So I took her with me, at the request of your Gram and Gramps. I was to keep her safe. I failed.

"The Cult of Aeodymus had managed to get their hands on the machine your Gramps built. I don't want to go into too many details — this story is still too fresh for me. But your mother became part of a new army of *Teth* that I was leading to stop the cult. It took years. They were on the run, unable to get the machine to work without a key component your Gramps had managed to hide or destroy — I never asked which. During this time your mother met your father, and then *you* happened, Sawyer. I was there when you were born. You wailed louder than most babies I'd met. Or so it seemed. And it was obvious, right from the start, that you were the one the knotwork had been shaped to create. Your mother knew it, even when you were in the womb. Of course, all *Teth* mothers think their baby might be 'the one.' But she was right. It *was* you. Even I could see it, with no knotwork ability whatsoever.

"Your mother made a hard choice, shortly after that. We tracked down the cult, and they had found an alternative to making the machine work. It was ugly — horrible, actually. It would give them just one chance, but that was too much for us to allow. So your mother handed you over to your grandparents, and she and your father joined the fight to stop the cult and prevent Aeodymus from escaping his prison.

"We were too late to prevent them from using that machine. They opened a path straight to the torn Layer, and already there were creatures pouring out of it when we arrived. Your father — he was a good man. Brave. He was part of the first wave, fighting back the monsters, holding the front so no more could escape. He was killed there. It tore your mother's heart. I watched her resolve grow. She would never let Aeodymus escape that Layer, not matter what it cost.

"And that's why she and the others used their abilities to bind themselves to the machine, to the wizards and cult members who were running it, and to the hole it had created in reality. They created what we've come to call a 'tuck' in the fabric of reality. It pinched off that spot, containing the portal, and once again trapping Aeodymus and his armies in the torn Layer. But the cost was high. Your mother, and the other brave souls who fought that day, were trapped in the tuck with them. And have been ever since. We have always thought they were gone, shredded or absorbed into the fabric of the torn Layer. As it turns out, that isn't true. And it's the most wonderful news I've heard in a long time."

ELEVEN | RESOLVE

Xander had been staring directly at me during the last bit of this story, as I learned the fate of my mother and father. I felt streams of hot tears running down my face. I had a headache. I felt pressure in my sinuses, behind my eyes. And, I realized, I felt a tightness in my chest and my gut. My hands were clenched into fists.

I looked at Gram and Gramps, who were both crying silently. Gramps had moved to sit beside Gram at some point, and had his arm around her. They looked over to me.

"Are you ok?" Gramps asked.

I nodded. "Yeah. I'm sorry, yeah, I'm ok."

"No need to be sorry, son. It's natural to feel what you're feeling."

"How do you know what I'm feeling?" I asked, with maybe too much emotion behind the question.

"You don't have to be able to read the knotwork to see that you're upset," he said, giving a small smile.

Gram reached out and grasped my hand, and squeezed. "It's ok, Sawyer."

I nodded, and looked at Xander. "Is that it?" I asked.

"There's always more," he said. "But I'm not hiding anything from you now. I'll tell you anything, if you ask. I'll tell you more stories about your mother, if you want."

I shook my head. "Not now. But yeah, I'd like that. My question is, what do we do? You think Aeodymus — his real body — is in the Shadow Strait, but what does that mean? We go find him and kill him?"

Xander shook his head. "No. At least, that's not what I had in mind, exactly. Almost the opposite. If the choice is to kill him or let the Omni be destroyed, then I don't see an alternative. But I think there's another way."

"What is it?" I asked.

He smiled. "I think the way to stop him is to give him a life."

"Give him a life?" Gramps asked. "What, make him over so he can be the cool kid at parties?"

"You are not sacrificing Sawyer to stop him!" Gram said, her jaw tight.

Xander shook his head. "You two just never let me have the dramatic pause. Ok, let me make this plain."

He stood up and smoothed his clothes. 8-Ball moved up and hovered near his left shoulder, and in the light from the window, Xander Travel actually looked sort of *epic*. After spending time with him, and in moments like these, I could see why Gram might be taken with him. He was an Exemplar, after all. If anyone was cool, he'd have to be the *root* of all cool. The *apotheosis* of cool.

I pushed the covers back and also stood, a bit shakily at first but then firming my stance, trying to match his as best I could. I was wearing a night shirt and a pair of pajama bottoms. My feet were bare. I had nothing else but the woven necklace. I was standing in front of him as just me. As much *me* as I could be. And it felt like the right thing to do.

Gram and Gramps also stood, holding hands with each other. Gram reached out and took my hand as well.

I wasn't sure why we were doing it, but it felt like it had to be done. It felt like a pivot point — the *beginning* of something.

"We are going to find Aeodymus, in that dark world," Xander said. "And Sawyer is going to rewrite his story."

Gram, Gramps, and I exchanged looks. "How?' I asked. "Can that even be done?"

Gram sighed. "It can," she said. "But it's forbidden. In fact, if I remember right, Xander, *you* were the one who forbid it. So why would you allow it now?"

"Because the consequence of rewriting someone's story in the knotwork, here in the Omni, is to cause tears and holes in the fabric of reality. But we won't *be* in the Omni."

We looked at each other again, surprised. I saw what he had in mind, and felt a sort of excitement, along with a wall of dread. "Because we'll be in the Dark Omni," I said. "You want me to tie him to the dark knotwork."

"He wants an omniverse to reshape in his image. We'll give him one. And if we do it right, we'll seal the gap between the two forever."

"But we don't even know if the 'Dark Omni' is a real thing," Gramps said. "We could be risking everything on your hunch."

"We know the dark knotwork exists," Xander said. "We know the In-Between exists. I'm convinced there *is* a Dark Omni. 8-Ball has more or less confirmed it."

"More or less?" Gramps asked.

"He's vague. But then, that would be an existence that 8-Ball isn't a part of. It might not be possible to confirm it."

We all stood quietly, thinking, wondering. "Ok," I said, finally.

"Sawyer ..." Gram started.

"This is a plan," I said. "Something to work toward. What's the alternative? Keep running, hopping from Layer to Layer, hoping to keep me away from Aeodymus forever? We don't know what the 'event' will be. This could be it."

Again, silence, until Gramps said, "He has a point, Liv. We're short on plans at the moment. We can't keep running."

"I know he's right!" Gram said. "I'm trying to think of a way to make him *not* right!"

"Until then," Xander said, "How about we try the plan of the most long-lived man in the room?"

"For now," Gram said, giving him a hard look. It was clear that over the past few days her "crush" on him had faded, replaced by resentment for putting me in danger. Looking at the knotwork, I could see the connection she had with Xander thinning a bit, while her link to Gramps remained strong. Maybe stronger than ever. I liked that, though part of me felt some sort of regret over it. I wasn't sure why. It may have been as simple as the fact that I *liked* Xander, and could understand why she might have loved him.

"I'll take it," Xander said. "So we'll make the journey to the Shadow Strait. It will take a while, so we have plenty of time to come up with an alternative plan."

"Take a while?" I asked. "Can't we just button there or something?"

Xander shook his head. "I'd prefer not to. At the moment we have the element of surprise. I'm reasonably sure, that with you removing the dark network from your braid, that we can button travel once again without being detected. But I'd rather play that as a last card, not the first. We'll take the long route. It'll be fun. There will be camping!"

"Joy," Gramps said.

"You *love* camping," Gram said.

"I love camping when I'm on a fishing trip," Gramps said. "Not thrilled about weeks on the road with Xander and his nuisance pal, 8-Ball."

"Well aren't you a ray of sunshine?" Xander asked, then smiled. He stepped up and between Gram and Gramps, putting his arms around their shoulders. Gramps put an arm around my shoulder, too. We all stood in a sort of group hug, and Xander said, "Let's go save the Omniverse."

And with that, we were ready to get to work.

HOW TO MAKE AN AUTHOR STUPID GRATEFUL

If you liked this book, there are two things you can do to keep the adventure going and to make yours truly a very happy and grateful author.

REVIEWS

Written reviews on Amazon and Goodreads are like oxygen for authors—we need them to live! So please, if you liked this book, consider reviewing it on both of these sites. Click below to go straight to their listings:

Sawyer Jackson and the Long Land on Amazon.com:
http://amzn.to/1IHji4a

Sawyer Jackson and the Long Land on Goodreads.com:
http://bit.ly/1GVPMFM

BECOME A SLINGER

If you liked this book, you'll probably love the rest of my work, too. I'd love to tell you all about it! Get on my mailing list to hear about new book releases, new blog posts, new podcasts, and any freebies, giveaways, and contests that come along. **Become a slinger at kevintumlinson.com**

TELL ME ALL ABOUT IT

I'd love to hear what you thought of the book (or *any* of my books). And I'm happy to answer questions, offer advice, or just shoot the breeze! Go to kevintumlinson.com/contact and send me an email. I'd love to get to know you!

ABOUT THE AUTHOR

Kevin Tumlinson was born in Wild Peach, Texas, during the early 70s. Which means he had practically nothing to do for the first 18 years of his life.

That meant he was free from outside stimulus, which gave him a creative edge. He spent his days roaming the back woods and open pastures and abandoned junk piles of Wild Peach, getting into a lot of trouble and building a rich inner world that comes in real handy today.

Kevin is the author of dozens of novels and novellas, including his popular *Citadel* science fiction trilogy and his ongoing *Sawyer Jackson* contemporary fantasy series.

Kevin was the winner of the Veterans of Foreign Wars Voice of Democracy award, as well as a two-time winner of the Danny Lee Lawrence Award for Fiction.

In addition to writing and publishing, Kevin is the host of the Wordslinger Podcast (wordslingerpodcast.com)—a weekly interview-format show in which Kevin talks to some of the most interesting and upwardly mobile entrepreneurs around. Kevin makes a regular habit of coaching and helping other authors, entrepreneurs and would-be authors improve their craft, build or grow their business, and generally just make their lives better through writing.

Kevin lives with his wife, Kara, in the Greater Houston area, but has a grand master plan to chuck it all and live as an RV nomad, exploring the world, chasing his travel muse, and creating stories from the grist he finds out there.

Visit Kevin at kevintumlinson.com for more information about his work, and to connect with him and become one of his Slingers. You can also follow him on Facebook (/kevintumlinson) and Twitter (@kevintumlinson). He is no longer responding to smoke signals, and apologizes for the inconvenience.

www.ingramcontent.com/pod-product-compliance
Lightning Source LLC
Chambersburg PA
CBHW030336180626
46810CB00003B/1377